to Lee, my fairy godmother,
With your magic you
helped me to turn a
ragtag manuscript into
a magical story!
I am sincerely thankful.
Blessings.

Light on Jib Island

Jan Gilley

Light on Jib Island

©2013 Janis Gilley

ISBN 13: 978-1-938883-66-8

Cover painting by P.W. Jostrom

Illustrations by Skye Sanderson

Designed and produced by
Maine Authors Publishing
558 Main Street, Rockland, Maine 04841
www.maineauthorspublishing.com

Manufactured in the United States of America

For Nana and for Mimi

But especially,

For PAPA

Preface

My great grandfather, Captain Isaiah Wallace, owned a schooner and sailed from Nova Scotia along the Maine coast to trade in New York. My grandfather, John Elis Sjostrom, was a Swedish merchant sailor who lost his life at sea at the end of World War I, when my father was five years old. My husband Roy is descended from generations of Maine lightkeepers, from William Gilley on Baker Island to Howard Gilley on Curtis Island. I always thought there should be a story in this connection that Roy and I have to sailors and lights, so I began to read accounts of real life on lighthouse islands. I especially enjoyed *Lighthouse in My Life* by Philmore Wass. The stories of lightkeeping families serving on the coast of Maine ignited my imagination.

As I walked with my border collies along the Rockland Breakwater one summer, I began to give voices, faces, and names to the children in my imagined lighthouse family. I listened to their conversations and, as the children talked to one another and to me, I was able to see how they lived and worked alongside their parents. I saw their joys, their struggles, and their adventures. Each child had responsibilities to their parents and to one other, and each had a clearly individual personality.

After doing further research about Maine lightkeepers of the early twentieth century, I began to put together the adventures of the Barton family, the lightkeepers who revealed themselves to me while I was walking the breakwater.

In this way, *Light on Jib Island* was born.

CONTENTS

CHAPTER ONE

Elizabeth

"Ouch!" cried Elizabeth, as she slammed the heavy bureau drawer on her icy fingertips. She stuck the throbbing fingers into her mouth to soothe them. With her other hand she grabbed a pair of woolen long johns from the floor where they had fallen. Then, in one quick movement, she dove back into her bed. Wrapping herself with the well-worn quilt that Nana had made for her, she pulled her socks up to her knees and then wiggled the long johns into place under her nightgown.

"There," she mumbled, still sucking on her tingling fingers and letting out her breath. "Now maybe I can get some sleep."

Elizabeth settled herself into the familiar indentation in her mattress, shielding herself as best she could from the frigid air that attacked from all sides of her bedroom in the lighthouse keeper's house on Jib Island. The great kitchen stove on the first floor did not send much heat to her room, even though Papa filled it full of coal each evening. Elizabeth rubbed her feet back and forth on the flannel sheets to help create a bit of heat from friction. Then she tucked her long skinny feet and long skinny legs up under her nightgown, doing her best to keep warm.

"Breathe slowly, Elizabeth, in and out, in and out," she said to herself in an effort to calm down and get to sleep. Her thoughts drifted back to a warm June day in Camden, where she had gazed into the window of the Village Shop looking for magazines with photographs of far off places.

*   *   *   *

The Bartons were a lighthouse-keeping family that took great pride in its work and responsibilities. However, at least once a year, when Papa had business on the mainland, the whole family was treated to an adventure. A trip to the mainland was a luxury for a family living on a small island off the coast of Maine. Elizabeth and her three brothers were thrilled to have a chance to visit Camden. The boat ride and a picnic lunch on the shore were always great fun, as was scrambling for penny candy at Dougherty's store.

"Please, may I have two cents worth of licorice," Thomas had called out, his eyes glued to the candy window.

"I'd like some licorice drops and a peppermint stick, please," said Francis.

"Francis, get me some Necco Wafers," said Harry. "I like the chocolate ones."

"Please?" asked Francis.

"Pleeeeese," said Harry.

"I am going to get red licorice," Elizabeth said to Mother as she waited her turn.

"We don't have much time to get over to Haskell's to get you some shoes, Elizabeth. Your father will be ready to go quite soon."

"I don't care to have new shoes, Mother," said Elizabeth, as she thought of the covers of the magazines on display.

If only she could buy the *National Geographic* with photos of exotic places on the cover, she would be in heaven. The cover of *Life* for August 1921 featured a young woman being instructed by a handsome naval officer about how to take a sighting with a sextant.

Papa has already begun to teach me how to use a sextant, she thought, but the naval officer was handsome.

The Saturday Evening Post celebrated the Fourth of July with a portrait of a young woman in a Revolutionary War uniform. Elizabeth laughed out loud and pointed to the covers.

"Mother, look! These magazines show that girls can do lots of things besides housework."

"Of course they can, Elizabeth, after they finish the dishes!" said Mother, as she tousled her daughter's hair and kept moving out the door and up the sidewalk.

Just then, instead of seeing magazines, Elizabeth was surprised to see her reflection looking back at her from the large store window. Her eyes scanned the deep-set brown eyes and brown wavy hair that were just like her mother's; the full bow lips, more like her father's; and the tall, gawky frame covered by a mid-calf navy dress with white buttons down the front and a white collar. It seemed an odd sight to a girl of twelve years who was seeing her whole self all at once for the first time.

Is this really me? she wondered as she turned away.

She turned and skipped along to catch up with her mother, who was heading into the shoe store. After they had settled on a pair of brown lace-up oxfords, which Elizabeth immediately put on, the two headed back toward the harbor to find the boys.

Elizabeth slapped her new shoes on the pavement. They began to rub blisters on her ankles as she moved on toward the wharf.

"There they are, Mother." Soon she and her mother had caught up with and passed the boys as they all headed for the dock.

"Look out where you're walking," Francis snapped. Her oldest brother had no tolerance for daydreaming. "Just 'cause you got new shoes, don't think you can walk all over people."

Francis needed new boots, but did not get them this trip. Elizabeth, though, would have traded her shoes for many other things more precious to her.

The children started to run when they saw Papa waiting for them near the dock. He smiled to see his family running toward him and reached out to help Mother with her packages.

"Would you like a piece of licorice?" Harry shouted as a bit of black goo escaped the corners of his mouth.

"Thanks, Harry," said Papa, as he took a piece and popped it into his mouth. Then he headed for the boat with Harry close behind.

"We need to get back. The seas are picking up and it won't be light much longer," said Papa.

*   *   *   *

The snap of the wind against her loose window casement snatched Elizabeth out of June in Camden and brought her back to the freezing air of November on Jib Island. She wriggled again under the blankets to find a warm place and squeezed her eyes, pretending to be in the warm winter sun somewhere in Brazil or maybe even Tahiti. Even her Nana's quilt didn't seem heavy enough in this cold.

It was the first cold night in a long time that she had slept without her grandmother. Nana was the kind of grandmother who made everything better. If you were cold, she helped warm you. If you were angry, she soothed you. If you were sad, she cheered you up.

Even though the room was dark and empty, Elizabeth could see the lighthouse light burning through the window, holding her to her island home. It was cold for November and Nana's absence seemed to lower the temperature even more, as the chill permeated her small frame. Nana was her protection from the chill and from the kind of aloneness an only daughter could feel in this family; however, Nana would not be back until spring.

Elizabeth couldn't stand to think about how long the winter would be. By the time she saw her grandmother again it would be 1922, and she would be thirteen years old. Each breath brought icy air deep into her lungs and she felt the snow drifts piling up inside—from her toes through her legs and into her body. The frozen air poked at her skin with every movement.

"It's freezin', Nana," she would have said, if Nana had been there.

"Never mind," Nana would have advised. "Think of that day last June when we thought we'd melt by the stove, tryin' t'get the dandelion greens canned. Mercy, what a day!"

Snuggled up to Nana, rubbing her arms and legs against Nana's thick flannel gown, she would have fallen asleep. Nana always made the bed warmer and sleep come more easily, as she hummed a hymn in the tiny bedroom. Nana's voice was soft as goose down, and it stroked her mind with feathered chords until sleep took her.

Tonight, through the window, Elizabeth could see the lighthouse light and the eerie glow it gave the sky: a nightlight of moonbeams, as the fog patches drifted in and out about the house and tower. Like Nana, the light always surrounded Elizabeth with comfort. Not as exciting as her dreams of far off places, but the comfort of her home and her place in the great, huge world.

Papa never failed to light the lamp one-half hour before sunset and to put it out one-half hour before sunrise. It shone into her window on the mainland side of Jib, and cast its broad beams out toward England.

The long arms of light stroked the rough North Atlantic like the arms of a strong swimmer taming the waves with their power. They stretched toward the east and toward the north and south of Jib Island. Of course, the light didn't reach England, but it did reach out far enough to warn ships away from the rocky Maine coast. The ships that sailed from Maine and Canada with cargoes of pulpwood, and back to Canada with freight from the southern states, the Caribbean and even South America, relied on these lights. Their captains watched for and counted on the lighthouses, which were distinguished by their different light signals, to get them through the treacherous waters and the rocky shoals off the Maine coast.

It was not stormy tonight, but Elizabeth listened to the sound of the foghorn with its long, low moan. The foghorn was new to Jib Island. Just a year ago they had used a fog bell, which was operated by a winding mechanism. Papa had allowed all the children to watch the lighthouse engineers install the new system and explained how the horn worked. The new foghorn was powered by a coal-fired engine and was called a Daboll Trumpet, named for its inventor, Celadon Leeds Daboll. The low howl of the horn sounded spooky to the children.

"Don't like it, Papa," said Harry, who was then only three years old. "It ith thcaaaary."

Papa laughed and took Harry in his arms. He blew a low moan in Harry's ear and asked,

"Am I thcaaary, Harry?"

"No, silly Papa."

"Then the new horn can't be thcaaary either, can it Harry? Just pretend it's me, blowing in your ear."

Papa put Harry down and tickled him.

Elizabeth hoped the next day would be bright and sunny. The children would all have their chores to do. Fourteen-year-old Francis always worked with the men. Thomas, who was ten, did odd jobs inside and outside, and Elizabeth worked in the kitchen with Mother. Harry did his best to get in the way. The chores would keep her mind off all the things that whirled around in her head tonight. She and her brothers would be so busy that the day would fly by. In a lighthouse family everyone worked.

Thomas always said, "This is a very, very important job," as he took it upon himself to be in charge during chore time, even bossing Elizabeth and Francis.

"We must make the house spotless," he insisted as he scrubbed the stairs down.

"Spotless," mimicked four-year-old Harry, with his brows knit together and lips pressed tight, dripping water on Thomas's clean wood steps.

The children knew that when they polished brass or carried oil, everything they did was for the smooth operation of the lighthouse station. Papa was quite serious when he talked about the responsibilities of a lighthouse family. His handsome face and strong shoulders were more noticeable in his navy blue lightkeeper's uniform with the shiny brass buttons. His round cap looked rather like the ones worn by train conductors with a flat top and a short, round beak that framed his straight nose and strong chin.

Elizabeth thought Papa the most handsome man she had ever seen. The ship's captain that she would marry would have to be as handsome as Papa and have eyes as blue as his, as well as the nose of a Greek god. Elizabeth had seen the pictures of Greek and Roman deities and knew that Papa's strong good looks came from another place and time. In Elizabeth's eyes, his perfection extended to all he was and all he did.

The children watched Papa's deep-sea eyes and listened as he told of shipwrecks caused by a failed light. Everyone worked on Jib Island to keep the equipment and buildings in perfect condition and to keep the light and horn running without fail.

"The boats need us," repeated Harry.

"The boats need you to get to bed, Harry, so that you can get up and do your jobs tomorrow," Mother said as she winked at the older children, while taking Harry by the hand up the stairs amid his protestations and their giggles.

"I am big. I can stay up like Thomas. I'm four," he said, holding up four fingers for all to see. "Four is big, not little."

Elizabeth thought about the day four years ago when Mother had brought Harry back to Jib from the mainland. He was already a month old and had fat, pink cheeks. Mother didn't have pink cheeks, though. Her hair had its first touches of gray. Her eyes were not sparkling, her steps were slower, and she had to rest at the top of the wooden stairs that led to the boat dock. Papa had told them about her illness, but Elizabeth wasn't sure what he was saying.

"Is she going to die?" Elizabeth asked. "Will she be back soon?" "Why is she so sick?"

Her brothers just sat on the kitchen benches and swung their feet and looked at the floor. Only Elizabeth pounded Papa with questions.

"I don't know, Lizzie," he'd said, trying to take her in his arms and comfort her as she swallowed her sobs, his own eyes glistening with tears held back. She refused his comfort.

"Mother wanted Harry, Lizzie," Papa said. "She says he's a beautiful baby and we'll all love him."

"I'll never love him if he comes here and Mother doesn't. I'll never, ever love him," Elizabeth screamed as she ran up to her room.

Nana had gone after her and she had let Nana hold her as she wept. Nana's arms encircled her heaving body.

"Your mother will be home, my Rosebud; she'll be home. With God's help, she'll be home. Now say your prayers with me for Mother, say your prayers."

It was Nana's prayers that brought Mother home with Harry that sunny, Sunday morning and, as sick as she looked to Elizabeth, Mother's smile said, "Everything will be all right."

The next morning Mother did her best to make a fresh start with Elizabeth. As she stirred the porridge on the stove she said, "Lizzie, set the table now, please, and after breakfast I need you to clean up the dishes, as I promised Papa that I would iron the lens cover this morning."

"Sure, Mother," Elizabeth said, eager to please her mother after her tantrum the evening before. "Of course you know Papa will say that you ironed it perfectly, once again." Mother and Elizabeth laughed at predictable Papa.

When he did say exactly that this morning and smiled and winked at Mother, giving her shoulders a squeeze before he took the cover out to the tower, Mother pretended to be unaffected by his praise and played at pushing him out the door.

The children giggled while Nana chuckled and said, "Blow on out the door, Mr. Windbag."

"Out the door," said Harry.

Nana knew all about the workings of the lighthouse too. Her husband had been lost at sea long ago when Papa had been just a boy; she knew why the light had to be run with perfection. Maybe a good lighthouse keeper could have saved her captain. But it was a futile thought.

Reliving these days helped Elizabeth to relax, and her bed felt a bit warmer. Her thoughts rolled back to the morning. She did miss Nana and grew sad as she remembered Nana's preparations for leaving.

Nana's black coat and hat had hung on the pegged clothes tree in the corner of Elizabeth's room, ready to go. In the summer, the clothes cast strange shadows as they covered the pegs, becoming spooks during the long evenings when Elizabeth went to bed before it was quite dark. They would name the shadows after the people in Boston who lived in Nana's neighborhood.

"Why, how do you do this evening, Mr. Codfish," Nana would say, referring to a grumpy old man who lived on the ground floor of her building and always complained about the weather, the condition of the streets, the taxes, the woman who lived above him, and just about anything else. "Homely as a codfish!" she'd described him.

"I do believe Mrs. Rosy Nosey is with us tonight, Nana," Elizabeth would declare, talking about the woman across from Nana's doorway, who watched everyone's comings and goings and reported on these with regularity to anyone who would listen. Nana thought that Mrs. Rosey Nosey was very free with her gossip.

"Did you know, Mrs. Barton," she had said to Nana once, "Mr. James has been seen walking in town with a lady? I think there might be a wedding soon."

Nana had replied that Mrs. Rosy Nosey needed to mind her own business.

Elizabeth imagined the tall building where her grandmother lived, with a wide sidewalk in front of it, street lamps that glowed all night, and a trolley car at the corner that could take her anywhere in Boston. She could picture it, although she had never been there. Next spring she would be allowed to go for a two-week visit to Boston, live in Nana's apartment and see all the sights. Papa had promised.

CHAPTER TWO

Nana's Departure

On the morning of Nana's departure, Elizabeth had helped her pack the suitcase with cotton dresses, long cotton stockings, and funny underwear. Elizabeth made sure that Nana took the pincushion she had made for her. It was a square cushion made from a scrap of white linen left from her mother's new dress collar. She had stuffed it with some cotton scraps that were too small for quilting and had embroidered Nana's initials, D. E. B. (Daisy Elizabeth Barton), and surrounded them with blue flowers. The initials were in script and had taken her a long time, using very small stitches. She had taken the B out twice, since her needle was not very obedient. When Nana unwrapped it, she pursed her lips and tried to stifle a smile.

"My dear, you shouldn't have done all this work for me," she said, as Elizabeth gave her a big hug to go along with the pincushion.

Nana continued to tighten her lips and remain serious.

"Really, my dear, you shouldn't have bothered doin' anything like this for me." Then she scooped Elizabeth up in a big hug and held her for a long time.

What Nana liked best was to make things for Elizabeth, her parents and brothers. She could do anything with a piece of cloth or a ball of yarn. A small piece of material could become a new dress for Elizabeth's doll in no time, and everyone had striped mittens made with yarn scraps. When they sat around the kitchen stove on a cold evening, the whole family would try to guess who would be the beneficiary of Nana's next project.

"It's for Thomas," Mother said, as the family watched Nana's face for a hint. "Nana knows his color is red."

"No, Hildy, it's for Francis," Papa teased. "The sleeves are already three feet long."

Everyone laughed, except for Francis, who tried to tuck his gangling, fourteen-year-old limbs under the table. No one knew for sure until it was done, because Nana had her tricks and could measure a length on one person and know just how it would fit another.

One morning, the red sweater appeared folded on Papa's chair and the children cheered as he pulled it on and it fit! Nana took the praise with modesty.

"Guess I should know the right size sweater for my only son, don't ya think?"

Papa wore that sweater on the coldest days, for it was the warmest and softest one he had. That particular morning had been one of the many wonderful times during Nana's visit. She gave life on Jib Island something that made Elizabeth warm and happy inside.

It would be strange to be without her for the winter. Nana hugged and kissed them all, even the squirming Harry, dabbed her eyes with her white handkerchief, and walked toward the boathouse. Elizabeth held her hand all the way.

"Nana, write me letters, won't you? And I'll write you, I promise."

"Mmm hmm, of course I will," replied Nana as she gave Elizabeth's hand a squeeze. "I'll tell you all about the excitement in Boston this winter."

"Tell me about Mrs. Donaldson's cat and all her kittens."

"Of course," said Nana.

Elizabeth didn't know Mrs. Donaldson or her cat, except through Nana's stories about how they kept the apartment house in an uproar by doing things like knocking over the bottles of delivered milk and drinking their fill before people were even awake. Elizabeth laughed out loud as she watched in her mind the milk-whiskered kittens scampering around the hallways chased by the broom-wielding Mr. Codfish. The picture was real to her, as were all the others Nana drew, such as the Boston Public Garden, the markets near Faneuil Hall, and the ships that came in and out of the harbor. The plays Nana had described at the Boston theaters continued to dance in Elizabeth's head in living color.

But the best pictures were those of Nana and her husband, Captain Isaiah Barton, so handsome in their sailing clothes, sailing to the islands of the Caribbean and beyond to ports in South America. She replayed these pictures over and over so that she could feel the warm tropical sun and squint as the flashing mirrors of the wave tips reflected in her eyes. She shivered on the deck as the crew fought for their lives against the fierce waves of the indiscriminate, enemy storms. She imagined relaxing in a deck chair with brilliant, tropical flowers woven into her hair, eating exotic fruit. She saw her white face and feet become ruddy and brown from the sun and wind.

But that morning on Jib Island, it was Papa who took Nana's suitcase and lifted it into the boat, having tied it with a string to keep it closed even if banged around by the baggage men on the train. He and Francis and Thomas were ready to take Nana to the mainland and get her to the train, which would take her all the way to Boston, where she spent each winter with Papa's sister, Sally. The trip would take almost all day. Nana said she couldn't take winter on the island, even though she had been born in Maine and had lived there for many years. It would be too cold for her, and staying in all the time would not be comfortable for her, either, as she insisted on walking several miles each day.

Elizabeth held on to Nana's hand as long as she could. She looked at the shiny, wrinkled hand and the plain gold band that was always on the third finger. Then she loosened her grip and let her fingers brush across the familiar palm before shoving her hands into her coat pockets to keep them warm.

"Come on, girl, give me one last peck," said Nana, as she pointed to her cheek. "Right here!"

Elizabeth reached up and placed a loud "smack" on her grandmother's cheek, and they both laughed.

As Nana straightened up, she glanced across the island.

"Sure is a nice sight, this place. I'll miss it this winter, and our walks, too. You take care of things now, Rosebud."

Elizabeth nodded, although she always resisted Nana's leaving.

Jib winters were just too fierce. Even her sturdy parents and her strong young brothers had a difficult time with Jib winters. She couldn't expect Nana to stay.

"I'll eat well, too. Do you think I'll get stronger, Nana?"

Elizabeth struggled with her thin frame, worrying that she might not become robust enough to be a sea captain's wife.

As if almost reading her mind, Nana said, "You take good care of yourself. Eat plenty of those biscuits this winter, and lots of fish and milk and eggs too. Next summer you might have some flesh on your bones."

In the spring, summer and fall, she and Nana walked the length of the island and back at least once a day. They went north from the Keeper's house, past the Assistant Keeper's house, where the Guptil family lived, across the fields, and up the path to the highest point on the island. From there they turned west-northwest to the edge of the small pond and around through the small blueberry patch to the high rocks on the north edge. They looked into the western and northern skies to try to guess the weather and watched the weathervane on the peak of the house to figure the direction of the wind and to see if they were in for a nor'easter. Nana smiled as she watched her only granddaughter climb along the rocks and search for treasure spat up from the sea.

In the hottest weather, they climbed down the path to Summer Beach. Elizabeth took off her shoes and socks and skipped in the frigid ocean, holding her dress up around her waist to avoid the salt spray. Nana scooped up some of the icy water and splashed it on her face and arms. She never went swimming, even when the whole family came to the beach for a picnic and Mother and Papa went in with the children. The water was not often warm enough for this kind of celebration, but once or twice on hot July days, they braved the paralyzing waves and laughed themselves silly, while their skin and lips turned purple and Nana fussed that everyone would "catch their death."

The morning Nana left, the water off Jib was gray and foamy white. *It won't be like this when I swim in Barbados,* Elizabeth thought to herself. *I will swim for miles and float on my back and watch the gulls. My captain will row along next to me to keep me safe.*

Ice grabbed at the rocks at the high tide mark and held fast to the oarlocks of the small boat in which Papa had placed Nana and her suit-case. Nana looked down beyond the boat and felt the cold wind blowing up from the sea on her uncovered face. She could see Elizabeth waiting by the boathouse, watching Mr. Guptil carefully lowering the govern-ment boat down the slip and into the surf.

The government boat was larger and safer than Papa's. He had started the engine while the boat was high above the water and then shut it off. He had to wait until the boat had cleared the rocks below before he could start it again. If the waves caught the boat just right, it might be smashed to pieces. Papa and the boys were skilled and knew the ways of the sea. Nana had tried not to look terrified as she held, white-knuckled, to her handbag.

"My son is not the sailor his father was," she had said once on an-other trip to the shore that had been particularly rough.

Papa replied, "If you recall, Mother, you never let your son go to sea!"

At this, Nana pursed her lips and shot him dark looks that said, "'Course not; I lost your father. Would I be fool enough to send you out to be lost, too?"

Today, it seemed as if it would be another rough ride. Nana looked so small sitting alone in her black coat and her best black hat. Papa wore his stern I-am-in-charge face, with his mustache lip clamped down on his bottom lip, as the boat began to be slapped about by the waves. It was a rough day, and the launching was a bit risky. Thomas and Francis grabbed the oars and rowed until Papa got the engine started. He suc-ceeded, took the tiller, and turned the gray boat toward the shore several miles away.

Elizabeth could see all the way to the small town, but the buildings next to the town dock were not even the size of the toys that Harry played with. She picked up the binoculars and watched the morning sun dance on the windows of the buildings, looking like sparks jumping through the square grate holes of the woodstove. The flag on the white pole at the wharf flew with the red and white stripes straight out in a southerly direction, flipping back and forth at the corners as if someone couldn't decide how to fold it.

Elizabeth watched Nana get smaller and smaller, making sure that she was safe, as if taking care of Nana could be done with her eyes. She knew that Papa would take Nana's arm and the boys would carry her suitcase as they walked up the road toward the Browns' house, where they kept their car. The Barton's weren't able to leave the island for more than a quick trip very often, but when they did, everyone loved to ride in Papa's car.

Elizabeth pictured in her mind how they would all get in the car and drive to the train station, and how Nana would climb on the big, dark green, passenger car and find a comfortable, red plush seat to sit on while the great black engine growled away from Rockland toward Boston.

There was nothing more to see but the sparkle leaving the windows on the mainland as the sun rose higher in the sky. It was then, as she looked out over the cliff and out over the empty waves, that Elizabeth realized her stomach hurt.

The pain was the same pain that she'd had when Papa got his arm caught in the boat winch, which required a trip to the mainland hospital. That pain stayed with her even after a call from the doctor telling Mother that everything would be fine. It stayed until she saw Papa coming through the whitecaps in the boat, waving with his good arm.

The pain was the same one that she'd had when Mother was rushed to the mainland before Harry was born. Elizabeth had known that Mother was not feeling well, but Mother had told her she would go in June and it was only April. Papa had taken her at first light and Elizabeth had clung to Nana when Papa told them all to pray for Mother.

And they must have been good prayers because in the spring of 1917 when Harry was born, he and Mother both survived. Nana had taken care of them all, and Elizabeth had confided in Nana about her stomach.

"Well, Rosebud, that's just worryin' pain. You'll just have to work that pain out now, so give me your hands on this bread dough and work it as hard as you can."

She was eight then, and she punched and pulled and beat that dough with all her eight-year-old strength, and the pain did fade some.

"Good bread comes from bad feelin's," said Nana, as she prepared to bite into a hot slice. "And this is some of the best I ever ate."

She winked at Elizabeth and tickled her and made her laugh with a big belly sound, then gave her the slice to chew and savor.

"Mmm, those must have been pretty bad feelin's," said Elizabeth as she tickled Nana back.

But Elizabeth hoped there'd be no more babies on Jib. Her mother had never seemed the same after Harry. She rested more and gave many of the small chores to Elizabeth.

Late one night, when Elizabeth couldn't sleep and was heading downstairs to find her mother, she had overheard her parents in the kitchen.

"I hope we don't have more children, Will; the doctor says it's not wise."

"I hope we don't either, as much as you do, but we have to have faith, Hildy; we have to accept what is given."

Elizabeth wondered what this meant and wondered why her parents sounded worried, and quietly went back up the stairs so as not to disturb them.

Today, when she saw them tie up the boat and leave the shoreline, Elizabeth was glad she at least had her mother, now that Nana had to go. She held her arms tightly around herself, turned, and walked up toward the high place past the fields, where she tried to get one last glimpse of the black coat and hat. The picture would have to last her until next spring, after the last ice floe left the bay.

The sky was a clear, autumn blue, the color of Harry's eyes. Two small clouds played tag in the wind over the hills in the west, and some geese honked harshly on their way south in what sounded like an argument over which route to follow.

"Follow the train," Elizabeth yelled at them. "Follow the train. It's going south."

Elizabeth inched her way back to the house so she would see no one that she would have to speak to. The tears in her eyes would flow even harder if she were asked about them. Her best friend was gone until next spring.

She wiped her hot cheeks with a corner of her petticoat and took the back way into the house, up the white outside stairs and in through the side door. She crossed the dining room and slipped through a corner of the kitchen, and then headed up the dark brown stairs to her room where Nana still existed in all the things they had made and done. Alone and still weeping, she visited with these treasures, hoping no one would call her away.

Elizabeth stood before her bureau, and in her tiny mirror watched her own sadness slide down her cheeks. Her brown eyes were dull, not flashing black like they were when she was furious with Francis, or sparkling chestnut like they were when Papa praised her, but dull brown-black, ringed with red lids. She tried to push the corners of her mouth up with her fingers and pinched her cheeks.

"No captain will want such a homely face. Cheerfulness is an essential quality." She heard her own voice in the empty room. She couldn't look anymore and turned away.

Without Nana, she was alone again. Of course, Papa and the boys would be back by suppertime, and Mother and Harry were down in the kitchen or outside around the house. But even with their company, the loneliness hung heavily inside Elizabeth's chest.

When Nana was around, they could talk about things the way she would have if she'd had a playmate. Nana knew all the things Elizabeth thought the most about. Nana knew that Elizabeth longed for a friend, a girl her own age to talk to and to dream with. She knew that Elizabeth hoped desperately to go to sea someday. As a girl, her only hope was to marry a captain, because girls didn't go to sea by themselves. But most of all Nana knew she wanted to be allowed to go to the mainland to a real school where she could study in classes with other children … and maybe even find a best friend.

Letting her parents know this was rather futile and unkind, because they couldn't help her, and Elizabeth didn't want her parents to think that she wasn't content on Jib with her family. And, really, she loved Jib and loved all the things they did together. She knew that they needed her on the island, but it would be so very wonderful to have a friend, even for a little while.

She so looked forward to spring when she would visit Nana in Boston and see that giant city. What would it be like to live in an apartment building with many other families and to walk to the store, instead of rowing? What would it be like to eat in a restaurant once a week the way Nana and Aunt Sally did? What would it be like to have a bouncy streetcar ride every day? What would it be like to have other girls her age to play with and talk to?

She'd read in books about girls who have best friends and who share secrets and make secret plans. It sounded splendid. On the other hand, it was just right in so many ways on Jib. Elizabeth loved the island and the sea; she loved her parents and even her brothers, sometimes. How could she be so happy on Jib and want so many other things? It didn't seem right to want everything.

Elizabeth could get lost in her worries and her longing for Nana, but the worries drifted out of her mind and the pain in her stomach subsided. Warmth crept around her like a cat circling a tree, hoping for a bird—tentative and unsteady at first, and then with great deliberateness. Her toes felt one with the flannel and her head soon filled with moon dust. Then, from deep within her, she heard Nana singing her evening song:

> *Now the day is over; night is drawing nigh.*
> *Shadows of the evening, steal across the sky.*
> *Savior, give the weary, calm and sweet repose;*
> *With Thy tenderest blessing, may our eyelids close.*

CHAPTER THREE

Blueberries

The day after Nana's departure was beautiful and fair, as was the next, and the day after that, with clear blue skies and only a puff or two of a white cloud. It was unusual for November, and everyone found new energy in the brilliance of the sun, despite the shortness of daylight. The higher temperatures allowed Papa to finish repairing the cog system, which was used to bring coal and other freight onto the island from the ships that delivered it.

Ice had covered the metal rails and chains during the cold snap, but now it melted into tiny streams of water, which ran down the rocks to the sea. The rails glistened in the sun, and the engine chugged away. The men from the boat, Papa, and Mr. Guptil all worked to keep the freight from slipping off the rails until all of it was unloaded.

The sun warmed Elizabeth too, as everyone was given relief from the bitter cold of the week before. She was full of energy as she helped her mother with the cooking and cleaning. She knew how to make the morning porridge and how to make biscuits.

"Lizzie, better make a double batch again today. Hunting always makes Papa and the boys hungry as bears, and they're going out to hunt ducks soon." Mother always referred to Francis and Thomas as "the boys."

"And cooking makes me hungry as a bear," added Harry, as he stretched around Elizabeth's arm to put his spoon into the batter.

"You're not cooking, baby brother. I am. Now scat!"

Harry wailed and climbed down from the bench.

"Lizzie, you can let him help a little. He loves to do what you do."

Mother had seemed tired in the past week, but she never lost her sweet and quiet way of dealing with the children. Elizabeth thought it best not to make things more difficult for her, so she let Harry help and kept her thoughts to herself.

Well, I can't wait till he can go with "the boys" and get out from under my feet, she thought as she let Harry stir in some milk. *He's not a boy yet, and he's not a baby, either, and he certainly isn't a little sister, though that's what Mother wants me to treat him like. He's just a plain nuisance. I wish I had my sister, instead. She would have been some company. She'd be about eight. That's kind of young, but a lot better than a four-year-old brother. She could play with him when I was busy, and then she and I could do sister things.*

There was a small tightening of her stomach as Elizabeth remembered her sister. Jenny had died of scarlet fever when Elizabeth was seven. They had both been sick, but Jenny was only three and wasn't strong enough. Her bouncy, talkative sister was so quiet in her fever. Jenny was taken to Mother's room, and Elizabeth was left alone in the room they'd shared. Elizabeth remembered waking up with Papa putting cool cloths on her forehead. It was mid-February and the doctor couldn't come, but there wasn't much he could have done. He gave Mother instructions over the telephone and she and Papa nursed the girls.

When Elizabeth's fever broke and she started to feel better, Papa told her about Jenny and she sobbed in his arms. She didn't think Papa understood what having a sister meant to her.

They buried Jenny in the family plot in Belfast on the mainland. It was a frigid day and the sea spray turned to ice as soon as it hit the little boat. Only Papa and Francis went. Mother stayed with Elizabeth and they cried together. She heaved a deep sigh. As Nana often told her, "Not much use thinking about what could have been; spend your time on what is."

Maybe there isn't much use, but I think of Jenny and miss her and picture her all grown up, sitting on my bed with me, talking about secrets you only share with a sister, thought Elizabeth.

"That was a big sigh, Lizzie," said Mother, who usually noticed the moods of her children. "Something got under your skin?"

She didn't want to hurt her mother, so she kept her thoughts of Jenny to herself.

"Nothing, really," she said. "I just would like to go hunting once."

"Me too," added Harry.

"Oh, I'm not sure you would, Lizzie. I went once. It's bad enough cleaning and cooking a duck when it's brought home, but try as I did, I couldn't pull the trigger and shoot one."

"You're probably right. I probably couldn't do it, either. I'd want to catch it and bring it home as a pet."

They both laughed and nodded heads, accepting their similarities. Harry had forgotten completely about the biscuits by this time and had found the toy crossbow that Papa had made for him. He was practicing by aiming at Scat, who was absolutely safe and knew it. The gray tiger cat was curled up behind the stove and managed only a bored glance at Harry, the brave hunter.

The fire in the stove was hot, making the lighthouse kitchen a cozy place. A long, dark, wooden table stretched the length and center of the kitchen. The soapstone sink was rectangular and deep and had a cast iron pump at one end that pulled water up from the cistern under the house. If they had a dry spell, they would have to put all the pots, pans and buckets out in the rain to collect rainwater for drinking. The family gathered here for each meal, but between meals it served as a worktable for projects and a desk for doing lessons.

Sitting at the table, Elizabeth could see out over the small yard and beyond to the great rocks that were the strength and foundation of the island. The white-painted stone lighthouse was anchored to the rocks. It was round and tapered up to the walkway at the top, which had a black rail trim. Inside the glass enclosure at the top was the room where the lamp and the lens were secured. A little door allowed people to go in and out onto the walkway, which circled the light. Her father would go to the light through a door at the base, climbing the circular staircase to the lamp room. Today, Mr. Guptil was taking care of things while Papa went hunting. But there was no worry with the sun shining brightly and the sea relatively calm.

Elizabeth stood at the table and mixed up the biscuits in the same place where she had been doing her arithmetic that morning. Mother held classes in the morning, directly after breakfast. Sometimes a traveling teacher, sent by the Lighthouse Service, came for a few weeks. When the teacher left, Mother was in charge of lessons, and they all followed the plans that had been left behind.

But schoolwork took only some of the morning, and that left the other hours to cook and sew and clean. At this same table, Elizabeth had learned from Mother and Nana how to can beans and dandelion greens when they were fresh in the summer, and to make jam and jelly from the berries they gathered.

On this early November morning as she cut the biscuits and readied the pan for baking, she thought about how good that blueberry jam was going to taste spread thick on the biscuits, hot from the oven. They'd picked the berries in August, on a day that looked much like today, but it was as hot as a day gets on the coast of Maine.

"Pa, why do we have to take Lizzie out berrying?" Elizabeth had overheard Francis say to Papa as they left to ready the boat. "Can't we take Thomas?"

"You know Lizzie loves to berry, Francis, and she hasn't had a turn to go off in quite a while. She's been helping your mother and grandmother with all the canning, and I think she deserves a day of berrying on the mountain. Now, I'm sure if you think about it, it's only fair. And besides, Lizzie is awfully good company."

Francis rolled his eyes, but he knew better than to argue. Lizzie was not his idea of good company. Sometimes she was when they played games, because she was smart and a good opponent. Francis enjoyed the challenge. She beat him more often than he would like, and Francis had a hard time playing with her again soon after his loss. One night she took him three games in a row in checkers and he had simply gotten up and stomped off to his room. He knew he wasn't being a good sport, but it was hard to take that kind of a beating at the hand of your little sister. Anyway, he knew she would bring a good lunch to the fields today, and that was some consolation.

"Hurry up, Lizzie," Francis called. He and Papa were ready with the boat.

She struggled down the path laden with lard pails and a large pot, too, being very optimistic about the yield. The pot contained their lunch: peanut butter sandwiches, a jar of cold tea and some sugar cookies. In addition, blueberries would be the best part of the meal.

Elizabeth was a sight waddling down the path to the boat. She had on some of Francis's old corduroy pants, rolled up five times. It was one of the few occasions when she was allowed to wear pants along with a flannel shirt and some boots that also belonged to Francis.

Mother had tied her hair up in a bandana, then looked at her shaking her head, as Nana said, "My land, if you don't look just like a boy." And indeed, she did look just like a boy.

"C'mon Lizzie; hurry up! Don't waste our time!" yelled Francis.

"Hold your horses. I didn't see you carry any of this stuff. What're you going to pick in, your boots?" she replied. "And what did you plan on for lunch, Francis?"

"Oh, just get going, will ya? Here, give me those buckets and get in."

She climbed on the boat and kept sputtering at Francis as it was lowered into the waves. The noise of the engine drowned out her chatter. Francis and Papa were too busy with the boat to notice her mouth moving up and down and her eyebrows scowling as they all took off toward the north.

Being on the water quickly soothed Elizabeth; it always did. Riding on the almost waveless sea was a treat she looked forward to, as the water around Jib was rarely this smooth and comfortable. Elizabeth felt like a bird skimming over the surface of the water. She leaned over the rails of the boat, feeling the light spray reach up to caress her arm and fingers. She twirled her hand to move the water in different directions and watched a rainbow creating itself in the warm air.

Elizabeth peered behind her and saw the lighthouse getting smaller and smaller. Out of its sight, she felt at the same time free and uneasy. Life on Jib was predictable in many ways. Whatever needed to be done for the light was done; it ruled their lives. Living on the mainland was not something she knew much about. She looked to the shore, towards the landing where Papa had taken Nana to get the train. When she got to

Boston to visit Nana, she'd learn about that other kind of life.

There was a spot, not far up the coast, where the deep blue hills came right down to the ocean. Papa knew Mr. Carey who owned the fields, and he had permission to pick when Mr. Carey was finished gathering all the berries he wanted. There were great rocks at the edge, but there was also a small beach where they could pull up the boat and tie it safely.

"I see it," cried Francis as they neared the spot. They slowed the boat and Papa steered toward the beach, watching for rocks. He knew the way in and, as soon as they felt the jar of the boat bottom hitting the sand, Francis clambered off, his long legs clearing the rail of the boat. He landed on the hard, gray sand and tumbled a little. He was not always the most coordinated boy, having grown much too fast that year. He righted himself, pulled the line attached to the bow and tied it to a small tree up past the edge of the beach.

Elizabeth threw the pails and pot out of the boat and watched as they hit the beach, where they plopped every which way in the sand. Eager to be off to the field, she jumped and caught the tip of her boot on the rail, slipping down and landing on her knee. Francis didn't often get a chance to tease anyone who was clumsier than he was, and he didn't miss this one.

"Try walking on your feet, Lizzie. We'll get to the field faster," he gleefully yelled from the top of a rock.

Elizabeth gathered her legs under her and pushed herself up, rubbing her thigh top, which had been stabbed by a large pointed rock. The pain pushed sharp and deep into her bone because she had little padding on her spindly legs.

"Don't speak too soon, Stilt Legs. I'm sure you'll find a flea to trip over pretty soon," she yelled back, never one to take an insult without a retort.

Papa ignored their sparring and let his children work their jealousies out for themselves. During Sunday night prayers, he'd talk about how they should treat each other kindly and love each other, but he ignored most of the daily banter, unless it seemed to him that someone was being mean or hurtful.

Today, he was tending to the boat engine and didn't even hear their comments. When he had put away all the equipment, he jumped from the boat and headed up the sand toward the rocks and the hillside where his children waited to race to the blueberries.

The fields covered the side of the hills in patches of light and dark green, with the browns and grays of rock outcroppings scattered here and there. The low blueberry growth gave the fields yet another color on this splendid August day. At a distance, the blues and greens mixed into an ocean shade that moved just a little in the soft breezes that slipped off the sea and climbed up the mountainside. The reddish leaves added a blush of pink and purple all over the hill. The puff-patch shadows of white clouds drew dappled ponies on the field as they pranced across the sky. Even in her eagerness to reach the fields, Elizabeth took time to enjoy the lushness of the hillside, the ocean and the sky. She breathed slowly, trying to imprint the picture on her brain and save it for the day in winter when she would need it.

They raced up the hill, Francis in the lead, but at least carrying his own pails. Elizabeth was laughing now in the chase and Papa was close behind them. The sun pushed its heat into the deepest parts of their bodies, making the children feel strong and well.

"Wow, c'mere Lizzie, look at these berries," called Francis from a high spot above some rocks. "It won't take long to fill the pails. Maybe we will have to use my boots, too!"

"Never seen blueberries this big," cried Elizabeth as she reached Francis. "The pickers must've missed this spot."

"All that spring rain," said their father, "always makes big berries and big apples and peaches and just about anything else that grows. Dig in." He threw a handful of the plump juicy berries into his mouth and closed his eyes. Elizabeth and Francis did, too, as they rolled the ripe fruit around with their tongues and kept their eyes closed just like Papa, tasting the sweetness as long as they could before swallowing.

"Okay, let's get going now and fill these buckets. First one to fill a pail gets to steer the boat home," Papa said with a big smile. Elizabeth and Francis looked at each other in amazement and then began to pick as fast as they could.

What could he be thinking? Elizabeth thought. *Papa never lets anyone steer the boat.* Her fingers were flying from the bushes to the pail. Then, she saw the shine of something pulled from behind her father's back. Papa had brought a small blueberry rake. The children had seen these in the hardware store in Camden, but they had never owned one.

"Francis, look!" Elizabeth called. Francis glanced up without slowing his pace. "Papa's fooled us. Look what he brought." Francis and Elizabeth watched their father pull the rake through the berry bush. He had several handfuls of berries caught in the trough above the metal fingers, which trapped the fruit and cut it from the bushes. He weeded out the leaves and pieces of the tiny branches and dropped his yield into the pail. The fat berries filled the bottom of the pail.

"Let me try that, Pa," pleaded Francis. "This is great; you try, Lizzie." Elizabeth grabbed the handle and pushed and pulled it through the bushes. She also was successful and had another idea. She held the new tool, ran to another part of the field with it, and started to rake as fast as she could.

"Hey, you can't use that, Lizzie. It's Pa's. That's not fair. You're sure to win with that."

Elizabeth looked up and saw her father laughing with his hands on his hips. It was a great, low, belly laugh, the kind that always had the whole family laughing along with him. Francis fell down and rolled in the field, and Elizabeth could hardly breathe from laughing. In a few minutes, Elizabeth brought the rake back to her father.

"We'll take turns," he said, "but I get to use it most of the time. After all, you have strong, young backs and can bend over longer."

"Yeah, and you don't want to take any chances that I'll be steering the boat home," Elizabeth replied. The laughing and the picking continued in earnest. After a short while they picked in silence, each left to private thoughts. Elizabeth thought about how surprised Mother and Nana would be when they saw all the berries, and she thought about the blueberry muffins and pancakes and jam they would enjoy. It wasn't too long before Francis broke the silence.

"Is it time for lunch yet?" he asked.

"It's always time for lunch by your clock, son." Papa grinned. "Let's pick a little longer. We've almost got these buckets full."

"I'm ready to eat anytime," added Elizabeth.

In another half hour they had filled all the containers they'd brought.

"Time to eat," declared Francis. They all sat down on a large out-crop of rock. Elizabeth produced the lunch and they were quiet again as they chewed on peanut butter sandwiches, made with thick slices of Mother's bread, and rolled bites of big flat sugar cookies on their tongues until they were disolved. They drank the cool, refreshing tea. The waves splashed against the rocks down at the foot of the hill and their little boat bobbed a bit, as the tide had risen since they arrived. There was no worry, though; the boat was anchored to the beach.

Elizabeth stretched out on her back and looked at the sky. She and Francis had taken off their flannel shirts and boots and socks and were soaking up the sun in their lightweight shirts with their pants rolled up to their knees. The perfection of the day relaxed her and she let her eyes wander, looking at nothing in particular. Just as she was almost asleep, or in a trance, a small, blue bird fluttered into her view. She watched it fly from bush to bush. Songbirds were not too common on Jib, as there was little protection for small creatures.

"Francis, Papa, shhh," she whispered and pointed to the bird. Francis was an avid birdwatcher, even though he hunted game birds.

"It's a bluebird," he said. "Look at his orange breast. Let's follow him and see if he has a nest and any babies." They quietly left their father on the rock and moved cautiously, following the bird. Elizabeth saw the swarm before Francis, because he was so intent on the bird and never once looked where he was walking. His big foot came down on the nest of ground bees before Elizabeth could scream out a warning. Instead, she grabbed at his belt and tried to pull him back from the angry little bees, buzzing wildly around Francis's bare leg.

"Get back," yelled Elizabeth. She had pulled off her shirt and was swatting the bees away from her brother. Francis could only scream.

"Head for the beach. C'mon, follow me," she said.

She deftly skipped from rock to rock all the way down to the beach, followed by her crying brother, flailing his arms and legs as he nearly flew to the water. The high tide had made a little pool a few feet deep in the sandy inlet and both children threw themselves into it, making great noisy splashes. They ducked even their heads in the frigid water until the bees gave up on them and flew away. Elizabeth pulled on her brother's arm.

"I think they're gone," she said. Francis was still howling. "Get out and sit on the beach." She helped him pull off his wet corduroys, heavy now and sticking to his skin. Their father had made his way down, bringing their shirts. The stings were all over Francis's leg and there were even a few on his arms and stomach.

Elizabeth pushed him down and scooped heaps of cool, wet sand onto his legs and arms and body. She kept making compresses of muddy sand and replacing each handful of sand, as it got too warm. Papa helped her and soon her brother was only whimpering.

"Owwww," he moaned.

Elizabeth kept watching the bites to see that they weren't swelling too much. She kept wiping off the old compresses and putting new ones on him. Francis seemed to relax a little and his moans became less frequent.

"The dirty little buggers," he said through clenched teeth.

"It looks like he's not allergic to them, Lizzie. I think he'll be all right," said Papa.

"We should keep him cool for a little while longer, I think," replied Elizabeth.

"We can't stay too much longer. The tide has turned and it's getting late. I'll go back and get the berries and you stay with Francis."

"Sure," said Elizabeth, "How do you feel?"

"Better," said Francis as he lifted his head from the sand. "Ohhh, I feel a little dizzy, though."

"That's 'cause you had so many stings. They gave you a real good dose of bee stuff. Lie still till Papa gets back."

Their father made two trips up to the field to get all the berries and the children's clothing. Elizabeth hadn't thought about the fact that she had nothing on but a light underwear vest, and was shivering when Papa handed her the flannel shirt.

"Oops!" she said, responding to her father's wink.

"I guess it was for a good cause, but you better cover up now. Let's get this shirt on Francis, too. His lips are turning blue with cold." Francis allowed Elizabeth to help him with his shirt.

"Thanks, Lizzie. I know you tried to keep me from getting stung as much as you could. Where'd you learn about putting cold sand on the stings? I didn't know that."

"In one of my books about the tropics. Someone got stung and they covered her with packs of mud. Wet sand was the next best thing."

"Thanks, again. I really mean it."

"Yeah, I know," she replied and smiled down at her big brother. "You are a mess, you know. Thomas will think up some great nickname for you now."

With Francis as warm as they could make him in soaked pants, but at least a dry shirt, he climbed into the boat and huddled down on the bottom. Papa stored the berries safely away and then started the engine while Elizabeth cast off the painter and jumped into the bow as she shoved the boat off the beach. Then she grabbed an oar and pushed the boat out farther to avoid hitting any rocks. It was much cooler on the way back, and Francis and Elizabeth huddled together and shivered in the wind.

*   *   *   *

"Papa's home, Papa's home." Harry's voice was raspy and low for a little boy, and could also be very loud.

Elizabeth's daydream vanished. She woke up to her November kitchen in a split second and realized that her biscuits were about done, just in time. *Wow*, she thought, *I didn't burn them!* There was always a great deal of commotion when the hunters returned. Sea birds were an important part of the family diet. Wild meat was essential during the winter when food was scarce.

"What did you get? What did you get?" Harry bounced from the floor to the bench and back down again. Then he ran to touch the birds gently with his pointer finger.

"We each got a sea duck, Harry. I got my first very own duck," Thomas said proudly, holding a beautiful, fat duck in the air for all to see. Francis held back showing his so Thomas could have the attention of the others.

"That target practice has really helped Thomas. Today his aim was nice and steady," said Papa. "And he's getting a lot quieter out there. Didn't wiggle around and scare off the game this time. I think he'll be a fine hunter."

"It's a beauty, Thomas," said Elizabeth.

"It really is a beauty," added Mother. "Now take it to the shed and dress it, proud hunter." Thomas's nose wrinkled up a little, but he led the way to the shed with Francis and Papa following, grinning and winking.

The duck would be for a later meal, after it was dressed and roasted. Supper that night was haddock from the salt barrel in the pantry, cooked with potatoes. Of course, there were also plenty of hot biscuits with blueberry jam.

Papa said grace. "Thank you, Lord, for our food and for our safety, and thank you for Thomas's very first duck, and a right fat one at that. Amen." Then he added, "Please pass those biscuits, Mother."

CHAPTER FOUR

Inspection

"Lizzie, Lizzie. Lizzie. We all overslept." said Papa shaking her shoulder. Papa's voice seemed very far away as Elizabeth's dream faded. Her eyes snapped open.

"What? What, Papa?"

"Mother's not feeling well and Harry is out of sorts this morning without her. I need you to take care of breakfast. I made the porridge, but Mr. Guptil is waiting for me at the light, so I have to go." Papa had Elizabeth's attention now.

"What's wrong with Mother, Papa?"

"Oh, just a bug. No doubt she'll be up later and feeling fine. How quick can you be?"

"Quick as a wink!"

Her father leaned over her, tousled her hair and gave her a wink. "That fast, ay? That's my girl." Then he patted her cheek and zipped out of her room and down the stairs two by two.

The November warm spell had lasted only a few days.

The freeze returned in earnest. Elizabeth hadn't been thinking too much about the weather. She had other things on her mind. It would soon be Thanksgiving and, only a month after that, Christmas. She thought of food and presents and making decorations; there was so much to prepare. This was the best time of year. Although these holidays were difficult to compare to the wonderful warmth of the hottest day of summer, when they went on a great picnic at Summer Beach nestled between the rocks near the tip of the island. Even so, Thanksgiving and

Christmas were quite splendid.

Papa and the boys always made sure there were plenty of game birds for the holiday dinners, which would be held midday, as all noon meals on Jib Island were dinners and evening meals were suppers. Elizabeth and Mother carefully made the special pies, always apple and squash. They took the best of the preserves from the pantry, especially cranberry and cherry, to serve along with the dinner. On both days they ate until they were stuffed. Papa brought store candy from the mainland and Mother made brown sugar fudge and pressed sugar cookies into stars and bells and candy canes.

The food was delicious, but it wasn't the food that made the days wonderful. Elizabeth looked forward to playing games and singing songs and hearing stories. But most of all she looked forward to the fun of surprises. Hers was a family that loved surprises.

It was Nana's way to have something for everyone at Christmas: a bit of candy, or a new sweater or a knitted hat with a design. Papa was very much like his mother. He loved to surprise his wife and children with a new story, or something he made, or an unexpected outing. Elizabeth was busy planning her own surprises. She was also spending some time with the Sears catalog, trying to decide what she would like the most, although she knew she didn't have much of a chance to have it. Everyone was secretive at this time of year in the Barton family, wondering what surprises were going to come their way.

On this cold November day there was no time to think about Christmas. Elizabeth bolted out of bed. She threw off her nightgown and over her long socks and longjohns, she threw on her blouse and skirt. She grabbed her shoes but didn't put them on, as they would take more time. The stairs and landings felt warmer as she made her way down to the kitchen. Harry sat alone at the table playing with his porridge. Scat, the cat, sat next to him on the bench, trying to figure out if Harry had anything in the bowl that would taste good. Harry was whimpering.

"I want Mother," he said with a sniffle and without looking up from his bowl. Elizabeth knew Harry was going to be a challenge this morning, so she tickled his ribs.

"But Harry, you have me this morning, and I'm going to let you help me make some muffins for Mother, to help her feel better."

"Really? You are? What kind? What kind? Cimmamon? How about blueberry? No, I want raisin."

Elizabeth picked up his spoon and got a mouthful of oatmeal ready for him. "Let's decide while you finish your porridge."

Having a mouthful didn't stop Harry from talking. "I fink we sood make cimmamon and waisin together and we should put them in the big muffin pans and we should …"

"Okay, Harry, we'll do that. Let's just get finished with the porridge and have a big glass of milk."

Elizabeth was worried about her mother. She hoped that this illness wouldn't last into the holidays. *What would they do if Mother were sick over the holidays? That was a selfish thought. It was ridiculous to worry. Mother was never sick for very long, except once in a while when she had a cold that lasted a week or so.*

Nana always said, "God made mothers out of pretty strong stuff." Elizabeth figured that Nana was probably right. But the holidays with a sick mother would be pretty terrible, all the same.

"One last bite, Harry."

"Then we make the cimmamom muffs, right?"

"Yup, then we make the muffins. How about counting out the raisins? Put them in little piles with five in each pile."

This was a trick Elizabeth had learned from Mother. If she could interest Harry in counting things, it would keep him busy for a few minutes.

"One, two, three …"

Elizabeth flew up the stairs and knocked softly on Mother's door. "Come in."

"It's me, Mother. Can I get you anything?"

"No, sweetheart. Papa's brought me some tea. I'm sure I'll be better soon. Thanks, dear."

"Okay, Mother. Call if you need anything."

"I will."

Elizabeth bounded down the stairs two at a time and found Harry still counting.

"Three, four, five. Look, I have lots of 'em."

"Wow, let's see. … You have eight piles. I think we need two more piles for the muffins," said Elizabeth, feeling much better after checking on Mother.

Just then Francis and Thomas came into the kitchen with fresh milk from the cows. They did the milking and then took the cows out to the pasture, and at night they brought them in to the small stable under the keeper's house and milked them again. The cows provided milk for both the Barton and the Guptil families. Mr. Guptil had a wife named Faith and two boys, Sam and Freddy, who lived in the smaller house on Jib, just a short distance from the Keeper's House. The Bartons liked the Guptils and all four adults worked together for the light and for their families.

When the children were small, Papa had to do everything, house chores and the light, but since the boys were older now, the chores fell to Francis and Thomas, as Papa was usually busy tending to the light and fixing or making something that the station needed.

"Where's Mother? Here's the milk," the boys thundered.

"Shhhhh. She's not feeling well." Acting as if she was in charge, she added, "Hey, get those muddy boots off before you come into this kitchen."

The boys knew she was right, but that didn't mean they had to obey.

"Who declared you the mother?" asked Thomas, while Francis backed out of the kitchen and took off his boots in the hallway.

"Anyone who wants to eat cinnamon muffins better declare me the mother."

"Well, that's different," said Thomas with a smile, and he retreated to the hallway.

Harry was dragging the large mixing bowl over to the table. It was yellow, a big earthenware bowl, and too heavy for him to pick up.

"Let's go, Lizzie," he said.

Elizabeth went to get things from the pantry. "Hold your horses, Harry. We have to get all the ingredients out. Let's see, flour, sugar, lard, eggs, oatmeal, baking powder, cinnamon, and the raisins you already have."

"Lots of raisins," said Harry. "And how about milk? Don't we need some milk?"

"Yes, and you can grease the muffin tins."

Harry took the waxed paper Elizabeth gave him, dipped it into the lard, and rubbed lard into each compartment of the muffin tin. He had helped Mother do this, and he knew he was an expert.

"When will they be done, Lizzie?" asked Thomas.

"About an hour. Why don't you get your books out and start your arithmetic?"

"Boy, you sure are sounding like the mother!" said Francis. He had taken the milk to the pantry, where there was a cold cupboard to keep it. Some of the milk they would drink right away and some would be left to settle so the cream could rise to the top. Mother would scoop the cream off, and they'd take turns pounding it into butter with the small hand churn. For holidays, they pressed it into wooden molds and cooled it in the cupboard. The buttermilk was used in cooking, but Papa also liked to drink it.

Elizabeth and Harry worked on the muffins, with Harry taking a turn to stir and Elizabeth trying to keep the batter from flying all over the kitchen. Thomas and Francis had gotten out their math books and were working on their figuring, all the time keeping an eye on the oven as the smell of cinnamon increasingly wafted through the house. Papa's boots stomped on the back steps, and in seconds he was in the kitchen.

"Better take off your boots, Pa, before Lizzie yells at you," said Francis.

"Yeah, she's declared herself the mother!" said Thomas.

"An' we makin' cimmamon muffs," added Harry with his mouth full of batter.

Papa looked at his boys and winked at Elizabeth as he took off his boots. "Well, now, aren't we all lucky to have Elizabeth to take care of things this morning. I sure could use a cinnamon muffin and a cup of tea before I have to go out again. Awful lot o' ice built up on the slip again. Have to get the rails free from the ice before the coal boat gets here. We can't have the job be more difficult that it needs to be. Hard to slide the freight up on an icy slip. It will fall off to the side, " he said to Elizabeth with a mischievous grin.

The supply boat came with regularity to bring coal to heat the house and kerosene for engines, especially the engine that made the fog-horn sound. That deep, soothing blast sounded whenever the fog was thick enough to block the light from the ships off the coast. To Elizabeth, it sounded like the mooing of a mother cow singing to a newborn calf, only much lower and much louder. She loved the sound.

Elizabeth took the muffins out of the oven. They looked like little brown mountains with ridges and crevices of sugar crystals. The sweet, sharp smell of cinnamon enveloped the room and tickled their noses. All eyes were on Elizabeth as she popped the muffins from the pan onto the cooling rack. As the hands began to reach out for her creations, she warned them all.

"Better wait a minute. That sugar is hot, and the raisins will burn your tongues for certain."

Papa grabbed, anyway, and juggled his muffin from hand to hand, pretending to be burned.

"Give that one to me, Papa," shrieked a giggling Harry.

"Mmmmm." The sound of satisfaction filled the kitchen. Papa sipped his tea and the children enjoyed a glass of fresh-from-the-cow milk. The quiet of the kitchen was broken with the buzz of the radiotele-phone.

Francis answered, "Jib Island Light."

The voice on the other end said, "Will Barton, please. This is Gree-ley Hughes in Rockland."

"Just a minute, sir." He motioned to his father, who got up and walked to the phone. "Pa, it's Mr. Hughes," Francis whispered.

Papa nodded to Francis, who sat down again. All eyes were on Papa.

"Yes, Greeley. Ayuh, ayuh. Thanks, Greeley. We'll be ready."

He put down the receiver and turned to the children. They were ready. They knew what he would say.

"Inspector Dodge is on his way."

"Guv'ment's comin'," said wide-eyed Harry in a loud whisper. Even

Harry was old enough to catch the excitement and anxiety of an official visit of the United States Lighthouse Service.

The "guv'ment" inspector always came unannounced. The keepers, however, had a system for calling each other to warn of his arrival. Not one of the inspectors had any visible signs of a sense of humor. They expected perfection in all areas of the lighthouse island. They looked at the light and horn and their operation, and they looked at the Keeper's house and his wife's housekeeping. Everything was checked from the pantry to the privy. The children were both enthusiastic and nervous when the inspector visited, but they were well trained and went into action when the call came. This morning they had a few hours to prepare. Even though the light and houses were kept in perfect shape day to day, there were some extra chores to be done at the last minute. Everyone knew what to do, especially Mother.

Thomas spoke first, "What are we going to do, Pa, with Mother sick?"

Elizabeth didn't give her father a chance. "I know what to do, Papa. I can take care of the house. I've done it with Mother enough times. Let me have Tom to help me."

Thomas wrinkled up his nose, shook his head and looked to his father to save him.

"That's my girl, Lizzie. Thomas, you do whatever she tells you to. We've got to have things as perfect as if Mother were in charge."

Thomas nodded in agreement, as he knew how important an inspection was. It was much more important than worrying about having to work for Elizabeth.

"Francis, you come out with me while I alert the Guptils, and then you can help us out at the light. The lens and brass will need some touching up. Harry, you do precisely what Lizzie says. No fussing. Do I make myself clear?"

"Yes, Papa," said Harry. "The guv'ment's comin', the guv'ment's comin.'" He ran shouting through the house as if sounding the alarm.

Francis laced up his boots and went out the door, down the steps, and out toward the Assistant Keeper's house.

"We've got two hours," called Papa as he went upstairs and put on his clean, pressed uniform with his overalls over it and then hurried to the light. Elizabeth was busy writing at the table. Thomas started to pick up the food from the table and put it all away. He carefully saved the half-eaten muffins, wrapping them in wax paper. He poured the glasses of milk into a pitcher and took it to the cold closet in the pantry. When he came out, Elizabeth handed him a piece of paper.

"That's all I can think of, Thomas. Maybe it's everything, but if you can remember more, just do it. You take the upstairs and I'll start here in the kitchen. Harry, you go into the living room with this duster and dust all the windowsills, tables, and all the mop boards. Remember, every couple of minutes take the duster out the back door and shake it."

Harry was thrilled to have been included. He saluted his sister, "Aye, aye, Captain Barton," and off he ran. Elizabeth smiled as she watched his chubby legs pound through the hallway. She looked out at the light and saw the men scurrying around. Then she sat down at the table and made a list up for herself:

1. Pantry: check all food to see it is stored properly and neatly.
2. Kitchen: clean wood box — no mess on the floor.
3. Shake Scat's bedding out.
4. Wipe down the radiotelephone.
5. Scrub out the sink.
6. Scrub the table and wipe the benches and chairs.
7. Clean the glasses from all the oil lamps.
8. Wash the windows with vinegar.
9. Scrub the floor.
10. Sweep the rain shed.

"This will take more than two hours," she said to herself, but she didn't waste any time and did one task at a time, just as Mother would have done.

Harry kept running back to the kitchen from the living room.

"I did the windowsills, Lizzie."

"Good, now the mop boards."

"Yes, sir." He'd salute and head back to the living room. Every time he completed a task, he reported back to his senior officer. In about half an hour Thomas was back in the kitchen reporting to Elizabeth.

"All the beds are made and I mopped underneath them."

"How about the window next to Harry's bed? Did you get all the finger marks?"

"Yep. And I straightened all his books in his book box, too."

"You did all the brass doorknobs?"

"Oh, no, I forgot. I'll get those now. Where's the polish?"

"It's in the lower left cabinet in the pantry. Hurry, Thomas, so you can help me with the kitchen floor."

Francis stuck his head in the back door. "We've sighted the Inspector's boat. Look out the window and you'll see it, too."

Elizabeth could see clearly through her just-cleaned windows. There was the large, black supply boat, the *Hibiscus*. Gray smoke puffed from its tall stack as it moved steadily toward Jib.

"We've got about twenty-five minutes." Francis was back outside in a flash, running back toward the light, where Papa had him cleaning brass trim.

Thomas ran down the stairs; he was breathless. "Okay, Lizzie, I'm ready." Elizabeth had filled the pail with hot water from the teakettle and mixed in some soap and cooler water. The top of the pail was frothy. She picked up a string mop that was a foot taller than Thomas and stuck it in the pail.

"Take the other end of this table, Thomas, and help me move it." They lifted the heavy table toward the wall. "Let's move the bench, now." She gave orders while she lifted the mop from the pail and twisted the thick mat of strings to get most of the soap and water out. Then she swung the large mop over the table and began mopping where the table had stood. They moved it back, and she cleaned in the corner and along the outside wall. When she finished one section, she and Thomas moved the table and benches and she started on another section. Thomas took rags made from old towels and wiped the section she had mopped.

The back door flew open. Francis said, wheezing, "He'll be at the landing. Five minutes." Elizabeth and Thomas stared wide-eyed at each other. They lifted the pail together, carried it outside behind the house, and emptied it. Lizzie snatched a messy dishtowel and straightened it. Thomas put the kettle back on the stove. "Harry, c'mere," Elizabeth yelled. He came running.

Elizabeth looked at her two brothers. Harry had indeed taken some dust off the mop boards and half of it had landed on him. She brushed him off, wiped his face, and ran her fingers through his hair to settle it down. "Pull up your socks," she said to Harry, who still wore short pants. "Thomas, wipe your face." She took a deep breath, wiped her own face, dried her hands on her apron, and hung it on the hook in the pantry. She put on her coat and buttoned Harry into his, smacked hats onto all their heads, and grabbed mittens. Then she led her brothers out the back door and over to the landing. Harry skipped all the way.

"The guv'ment's comin', the guv'ment's comin'," he sang in a breathy whisper as he approached the landing.

Papa looked stern as he took charge of the levers that controlled the donkey engine that powered the winch that pulled the yawl boat that had been lowered from the *Hibiscus*. The mate from the larger boat was in charge of the yawl boat, and he ran it full ahead toward the slip at Jib. He hit the slip and slid halfway up on the slip's stringers, and then gave Papa the signal to engage the winch to pull the boat all the way up to the top of the cliff. When the yawl boat was secure, Papa took off his coveralls and the white glove he wore to keep engine grease off his hands. In his uniform, with brass buttons shined and dazzling like little suns, he greeted Inspector Dodge. The two men shook hands while the children watched.

Papa gave Elizabeth a quick wink as he turned to escort the inspector to the house. Papa walked close to Inspector Dodge and the children tried to hear the conversation as they climbed the stairs. "Hildy has had a bad case of the flu and is in bed. I hope you won't mind not disturbing our room."

"That's too bad, Barton. How long has she been ill?" asked the inspector.

"She hasn't been feeling well for a week or so, but it got much worse last night."

The Barton and Guptil children followed up to the house and

stood quietly outside, waiting for the inspector to look over the kitchen and pantry, then the dining room and living room, and finally the second floor. The inspector looked at the children's bedrooms and the attic room, where the schoolteacher stayed when she came for her visits. He checked the mop boards and the windows and looked to see if the closets were tidy. He said a little, mumbling "mmmm" from time to time. He ran his finger over the bookcases looking for dust and glanced at the shiny doorknobs.

"The house looks splendid, Barton. Who did all the work this morning?"

"Why, the children did. Elizabeth supervised; she knows what to do. Hildy has taught all of them how to take care of the house."

"She has done the job well, Barton. Your wife and children are a credit to you, young man. Just the kind of family a keeper needs." Then he added, as he came back down to the kitchen, "Yes, a terrific light station family. Do I smell cinnamon?" he asked as he looked at Elizabeth, Francis, Thomas, and Harry, still lined up by the back porch.

"Yes, sir," said Papa. "Elizabeth made muffins this morning. Would you like one?"

"I think I will have to sample them, Barton, for a full inspection!"

When the inspector finished his muffin, he said, "Good work, children. You have done a fine job today! Wonderful muffins."

Harry saluted him, and everyone, including the inspector, burst out laughing. He gave Harry a pat on his blond head. "Are you going to join the Lighthouse Service when you grow up, young man?"

"Yes, sir," said Harry without hesitation.

Papa beamed with pride. Then he and the inspector went out the kitchen door and walked down toward the landing, deep in conversation. The sailors from the *Hibiscus* were not quite through unloading. The yawl boat had made more trips back to the *Hibiscus* to get supplies for the island, and the sailors had carried the coal to the shed where it was stored. They ran through the boathouse and over to the pile with the heavy loads of coal on their backs, and then opened their bags and dumped the coal. Thomas and Harry ran down to watch them and stayed to wave goodbye to the *Hibiscus*.

When the yawl boat left for the last time and the inspector was well out of earshot, the children gave a wild whoop. Francis picked up Harry and tickled his stomach until Harry could take no more. Elizabeth whispered to Thomas, and they all ran back to the kitchen. Thomas went into the pantry and came back with a jug of milk. By the time he returned, Elizabeth had the morning muffins out on the table.

"C'mon, everyone; we need a snack."

"We sure do," added Thomas.

"Me, especially," said Francis. "I never polished so much brass in such a short time. I'm bushed."

"You?" cried Thomas. "We did this whole house in no time."

The children went on and on about their accomplishments, each one exaggerating until their bragging became ridiculous.

"I had to move the entire mouse family that lives behind my closet and relocate them temporarily to the woodshed," Thomas said, winking at Elizabeth and stuffing a muffin in his mouth. "You know, they have a lot of furniture, and now I suppose they expect me to help them move back."

Francis reached over and knocked Thomas off the bench.

"Can I go see their house, Thomas? Can I? Can I?" howled Harry.

Just as things were about as noisy as could be, the children heard a familiar voice.

"What is happening down here?" said Mother softly. She was standing at the bottom of the stairs in her bathrobe, not looking well at all.

Francis jumped up. "Mother, we woke you. We're sorry, really."

"Yes, we are," added Elizabeth and Thomas.

Harry ran over and grabbed his mother's bathrobe while Francis pushed the rocking chair under her.

"The guv'ment came," blurted out Harry.

The others spoke at the same time. "And we did an excellent job. We passed inspection. He said we were terrific. We did all the cleaning. And now we're celebrating with muffins Lizzie made."

"And I made, too!" said Harry.

"Shhh, slow down and tell me all about it, one at a time."

Harry curled up in Mother's lap and the others sat down on the bench and told her everything that had happened. Mother's otherwise pale face beamed at her children and she patted Harry's back as they gave their account of the morning.

The kitchen was warm from the stove and the winter sun streamed through the sparkling windows. Scat, who had watched the whole episode from his place behind the stove, now stretched and sauntered over to the bench and hopped up looking for a muffin crumb or two or a bit of milk to lap. He found just what he was looking for because the children's attention was completely taken by their discussion with Mother, who "oohed" and "aahed" in just the right places.

CHAPTER FIVE

Miss Honey

Aweek after the inspection, Papa and Francis had taken the boat over to the mainland to pick up the new teacher. It was a clear November day, but the sea was choppy as Papa steered the government boat back toward the dock at Jib. The children watched anxiously to see their teacher, who would stay for a month and then come back for another month in the late winter. The rest of the school year they would work with Mother on lessons that the teacher left for them. As the boat approached, Elizabeth saw a young woman sitting bundled up in the bow of the boat with bags and boxes piled around her. Francis was in the middle and Papa was in the stern holding the rudder. The spray flew up around the sides of the boat as it pounded through the waves.

In only a few minutes the boat docked and the young woman grabbed the rope railing and climbed the wooden planking. She smiled as she came toward Mother, Elizabeth, Thomas, and Harry, who were eager to greet her. She was dressed in a long black coat with many small black buttons and a thick woolen shawl that covered her face, all but her eyes. They were kindly eyes, bright and green. A few wisps of straw colored hair flew around her face as she unwound the shawl to say hello in a rich, low voice. A lovely dimple decorated the center of each cheek when she smiled at the children.

Elizabeth was taken with her right away. Mother watched as Elizabeth welcomed her new teacher.

"Hello," she said. "I am Elizabeth and these are my brothers, Thomas and Harry."

"Hello," said the young woman as she stretched out her hand to shake first Elizabeth's and then Harry's and Thomas's.

"I am Anastasia Honey. I am so glad to meet you. I have heard a great deal about Jib from the teacher you had before me, Miss Anita. She told me that you are an excellent student, Elizabeth, and your brothers are as well."

Elizabeth, looking at the ground, smiled and said a quiet "Thank you."

Thomas inserted, with too much honesty, "She was telling the truth about Lizzie and me, but not about Francis. He doesn't like school."

"Well, we'll see if we can help him like it this year," replied Miss Honey.

"I'm a wondruful studett too," said Harry, pulling on Miss Honey's skirt, wishing to be included.

"Of course you are, Harry," said Mother.

"Is your real name Honey?" asked Harry.

"Yes, it is, and you may call me Miss Honey."

"I love honey!" said a giggling Harry.

"Welcome to Jib, Miss Honey. I'm Hildy Barton."

"I am very happy to be here," said Miss Honey. "I have heard such good things about your family."

"Thank you," said Mother. "I hope you think the same when it's time to go." They laughed together.

Papa and Francis joined them and Papa rushed them all out of the cold wind and into the house for dinner. Papa and Francis carried Miss Honey's bags and boxes up to the attic where she would stay, and left them to be unpacked later.

At dinner, Miss Honey said to Papa, "I prefer to be called Anna by you and Mrs. Barton. And I will be Miss Honey to the children. Anna is my nickname. My father is a navigator on a large ship, and he met my mother in Russia and brought her back as his bride. So I have a Russian first name and an American last name."

"That's sooo romantic," said Elizabeth, as the boys made silly faces. "Where are you from? Where do you live when you are not teaching?"

"We have always lived in New York City on the Lower East Side near the river. I have two brothers, who have gone to sea, and now I go to the islands! My mother is alone some of the time when my father is gone, too. But she is a seamstress and is usually very busy."

"Did she make your beautiful coat?" asked Hildy.

"She makes all my clothes, and I am very grateful. She insisted that I stay in high school and then go to normal school to become a teacher. I love teaching, so I guess she was right. The Lighthouse Service has just hired me, and you are my first students. I am so excited!"

"We're excited too!" said Harry. "I'm going to learn to read and I can't wait!"

Everyone had a good laugh at Harry's enthusiasm, and the children watched Miss Honey intently for the rest of the meal. Her hair was a bit wispy and curly around her face. She had skin the color of ripe peaches and was plump enough to have a good sturdy lap for sitting on. Harry discovered this right away as he wiggled his way to her during dinner. After dinner, she reached down and lifted him onto her lap. Harry was in love!

Papa began to speak of school business after dinner. "Thomas will begin grade five work this year, although he is quite ready for grade six reading and he loves history and geography."

Thomas nodded in agreement. "Could we read *Treasure Island* by Robert Louis Stevenson?" he asked.

"You've read that a hundred times," said Elizabeth, sighing.

Papa looked around at the children, his eyes calling for silence as he continued. "Francis will be taking his high school entrance examinations this spring. He needs to be prepared for those. I believe you have been given the required areas of study?"

"Yes," replied Miss Honey. "I have the materials we need to get him started. I'll set up a program for him to follow through the winter. When I return in January, I'll see him through the final review and prepare him for the tests."

Francis looked at the floor. Elizabeth knew he was not eager to begin schoolwork again. He would much rather go hunting or fishing, as his lobster traps were bringing in quite a good catch each week and needed constant repair. His sister knew there were a great many things he'd rather do besides go to school.

Elizabeth listened to the grownups talk about the high school entrance examinations. As much as Francis didn't want to go, she was eager to attend high school herself, and would go in a moment.

I can do the work as well as Francis, she thought. *I had better ask Papa right now to be given a chance.*

"Papa, I'd like to study the same work as Francis and try the tests too. I think I can do it and I want to go off when Francis goes."

Papa eyed her with surprise. "Little one, slow down. I don't know if you are ready to go off to the mainland yet. Don't be in too much of a rush."

"But, Papa, Francis and I were in the same math book last year and I was only a few chapters behind him. I can read as well and my handwriting is better!" She threw a self-satisfied glance in Francis's direction as he continued to look at the floor.

"I know how quick and able you are, Elizabeth, but there is something to be said for time, and I believe you need time here with the family before you go off. Francis is older and should be ready to go."

Mother said, "I don't think I am ready to part with you just yet, Elizabeth. You are my only girl. You wouldn't leave me here on Jib with just Papa and Thomas and Harry?"

She ignored her mother. "Will you let me try the tests, Papa? And if I pass will you think about letting me go? Will you?"

Francis, most often silent, spoke. "Lizzie, you can take them and you can take my place at the mainland school, too. I don't care if I ever go. I'll stay here and help."

Mother and Papa exchanged glances. Mother seemed worried and Papa looked stern. "Francis! You will take the exams and go to high school. You must have education for the future. There won't be many jobs for those who haven't completed high school, and college would be a very good idea."

"Now Lizzie," Papa said. Elizabeth sat on the edge of her chair, gripping the seat with both hands. Father took a deep breath that kept her in great suspense. "You may prepare and take the examinations, child, but I am not promising I'll let you go. We'll have to see."

For Elizabeth, Papa's reply was a victory. She was certain that she could convince him and her brain was already buzzing with plans to study as hard as she could and pass the examinations.

Miss Honey spoke. "I will test you both tomorrow and we'll see where to begin."

"Harry looked up at her with adoring eyes, "Will you test me, too? I know my numbers and I can write an 'H' for Harry."

"That's terrific, Harry," said Miss Honey. 'H' is for Harry and it also is the first letter of Honey."

Harry's grin spread all over his round little face.

Mother said, "Harry would like to go to school, too, but it's not time yet. He will be ready next year."

"I'm big, Mother. I'm big. I want Miss Honey to teach me, too!" said a tearful Harry.

Miss Honey winked at Mother. "Well, Harry, if you are a very good boy for your mother each morning, she can send you up to the schoolroom at 11 when your brothers and sister are finishing their lessons for the morning. We can spend a little time learning letters. How would you like that?"

Harry wiped his eyes and looked to Mother for approval. She nodded her head and his bright smile returned.

"If he's any trouble in the schoolroom, you will send him down, won't you, Miss Honey?" chimed in Thomas.

"I don't think he'll be any trouble," she answered. "What do you think, Harry?"

Harry shook his head from side to side. "No, I won't be trouble, I won't."

The adults moved into the living room and finished their discussion about school matters and life on Jib Island. When all the school matters were taken care of, Papa called the children in and Miss Honey offered to help Elizabeth and Thomas with the dishes. Mother said that she and Francis would do them that night so Elizabeth and Thomas could help her unpack things in the attic. Francis looked very unhappy as he began to clear the table, but Elizabeth and Thomas just about bounced up the stairs.

"What about me?" cried Harry.

"Harry, I need you to help me at the light tonight," said Papa, "so get your coat on." This seemed to satisfy the four-year-old, and he ran for his coat.

In the attic, Elizabeth and Thomas asked Miss Honey question after question. They thought of all the things to ask that their parents might not have let them ask.

"What books have you brought?" asked Elizabeth. "Are you going to read to us?"

"How long will you stay here? Where are you going after Jib?" asked Thomas.

Would the older Guptil boy be starting school? Why did she become a teacher? Was she going to get married? Had she been to sea? Did she get seasick? Would she like to walk around Jib? Would she like to go duck hunting with them? The questions continued on and on.

She had brought lots of books—schoolbooks and reading books and even a new atlas of the world. She also brought the curriculum guides for each grade and some practice examination books.

Miss Honey looked at Elizabeth and Thomas.

"Have you read *Little Women* and *Jane Eyre*? What about *Huckleberry Finn* and *Tom Sawyer*?" she asked.

"I promise I will read to you every day and I will stay for a month." The children looked at each other and smiled. "Then I am to go to Libby Island."

Miss Honey went on to answer just about all of their questions. "I will be teaching the older Guptil boy as well. I teach because I love to learn and I love children. I do hope to be married someday and have children of my own. Yes, I went to sea with my father once and got seasick. I would rather walk around Jib than sail around it. NOOOO, I do not want to go duck hunting, but I would love to see all the plant life on Jib and make a record book of all I see here. Whew, you ask a lot of questions!

"All right, children. All the books are in place and we are set for school to start tomorrow. Let's go to the kitchen so you can make me a huge cup of tea!"

Thomas and Elizabeth gave each other a smile of pure pleasure and took the stairs two at a time on the way down. Francis had finished the dishes and was sitting in a corner cleaning his gun.

"Are you all settled?" asked Mother.

"Thomas and Elizabeth were excellent help and we are all set for tomorrow."

"I spoke to Mrs. Guptil and she will be sending Sam over at nine."

"That's fine. We'll begin at nine so the children will have time to get their morning chores out of the way," said Miss Honey.

This last remark did not get an enthusiastic response; nor did the next.

"Time for bed, children." said Mother.

Just then, Harry flew in the door. "I helped Papa with the light, Mother. I can almost do it myself, really, I can. Right, Papa?"

"You were a great help Harry, my boy. Only a few more inches and you can fill the kerosene yourself," said Papa. "But now it must be time for bed."

"If you don't mind," said Miss Honey, "I'd like to start a tradition for this month that I am here. I'd like to read aloud to everyone for just a little while before bed, if that's all right."

"That's splendid," said Thomas. "Can we read *Kidnapped*? I saw you had it with your books. I'll go and get it."

"I'd rather you read *Jo's Boys*," said Elizabeth, looking sullen.

"Why don't we read *Kidnapped* first and then go on to *Jo's Boys* next?" suggested Miss Honey.

"Yeah," yelled Thomas, as he bounded up the stairs to get the book.

Miss Honey opened the book and began to read. She had a strong voice, read with feeling, and was a bit dramatic. Papa and Mother looked at each other as if their eyes were saying, "This is quite a treat for us, as well."

CHAPTER SIX

The Difficulties

School was exciting with Miss Honey. So, every day Elizabeth rushed through her morning chores of breakfast dishes and kitchen tasks. It seemed that there was more to do each day than the day before. Gathering the wash took more time than the previous Monday. The pantry counters seemed to be dirtier. And, indeed, the boys tracked more dirt into the kitchen.

Thomas rushed through chores as well. Many trips to the coal bin kept him from getting up to the schoolroom in good time. Thomas bounded up the stairs just as the kitchen clock struck nine and found that Sam Guptil was already working with Miss Honey.

The attic schoolroom, in the unfinished section of the second floor, was large and surrounded by windows set in dormers. They were high up so it was easy to see the sky but not easy to see anything else. When he had a short break from his studies, Thomas sometimes stood on his tiptoes and walked clockwise around the room to each set of windows, so that he could see all over the island. It was about three-quarters of a mile from where the lighthouse stood on the southeast tip to the rocks shading Summer Beach at the other end. There were several paths worn from one end to the other. The house was opposite the lighthouse and connected to it by a path and some wooden walkways with railings. It was built into the cliff and there was a long drop to the ocean. The walkways led down to the boat launch on the west side of the island toward the land. The big boats, like the supply and coal boats, came in north of the lighthouse where the cog and rail setup allowed for unloading up the steep bank. But Thomas couldn't see this area from the house very well, as the lighthouse was in the way.

Beyond the gardens, toward Summer Beach, was an area of grassy land for the two cows that provided milk for both families. The garden beds, now dormant, and an herb garden were fenced off so the cows wouldn't raid them. The supply boat brought hay to feed the cows during the winter and although they went out sometimes, they were comfortable in the small stable under the house.

Tucked up next to the house was the chicken coop. Gathering eggs was not one of Thomas's favorite chores. Gertrude, the largest hen, pecked him mercilessly. But he loved it when they had new little chicks, which felt downy soft as they squirmed in his hands. Harry especially loved the little chicks and could play with them for hours. Thomas knew all the island's paths and said he could walk across it blindfolded. Once he bragged about this skill to Nana, who laughed and said, "Uh-huh, I want to be there when you fall into the raspberry patch!"

This morning, Thomas was already working on his arithmetic when Francis, who had been detained by chores until nine-thirty, entered the room in slow motion, apologized for his tardiness, took out his history book, which was his favorite subject, and began working.

Miss Honey started her morning working with Thomas and Sam. She had a reading lesson with these boys and then she set them to some arithmetic from the previous day's lesson while she coached Elizabeth and Francis on grammar and spelling. Francis tolerated Elizabeth's inclusion in his lessons, and she was wise enough not to irritate him, fearing that Papa might take away her privilege. But she did like to keep the lesson moving.

"The parts of speech are: nouns, pronouns, verbs, adjectives, adverbs, prepositions, conjunctions and, and …" said Francis slowly.

"Interjections!" Elizabeth chimed in as Francis scowled, face down toward the desk.

"Good!" said Miss Honey. "What a great team you are. It's fine to help each other during class or studying, just not during the exam. Your homework will be to find all the prepositional phrases on page twenty-eight in your reader."

At eleven o'clock precisely, when all four children were hard at work on tasks from morning lessons, Harry appeared at the schoolroom door and waited until Miss Honey beckoned him to come up to her desk. He carried a small slate and a piece of chalk and wiggled a little while he tried hard to stand still. He whispered to Miss Honey.

"I've been practicing letters, Miss Honey. Did I get them right? Look, H, A, R, R, and Y."

"Beautiful, Harry," she said as he beamed an angelic smile. "Let's work on this 'Y' a little more. He's a fussy little letter who likes to be straight and neat. He's the first letter in 'Yes' and 'Yellow.'"

"And the last letter in Harry!" he said.

"That's right! And the last letter in Honey, too!" They both giggled.

Francis looked up at Harry and frowned. It was difficult enough to concentrate on grammar without Harry's giggling. He just wanted to finish and get down to dinner. Then only an hour more and he would have to be excused for some hunting or checking of lobster traps before dark. He did not know why he had to go away to high school. He had told Papa that he did not care about the Civil War when he had traps to set and mend.

"It just doesn't make any sense, Papa, because I am never going to need the Civil War for anything when I grow up. It's not anything I will ever think about."

"Well, you might want to think about the fact that your grandfather ran blockades during the Civil War, and lived to tell about it!" Papa said.

At last, the smell of fishcakes and potatoes came drifting up the stairs to the attic. Miss Honey dismissed them at precisely 11:30 a.m. so they could wash before dinner. Dinner began at 11:45 and was over at 12:15. They would be back in the schoolroom from 12:30 until 2, except for Francis, who left at 1:30 to take care of his traps.

On bright, sunny days, when the wind was not too fierce, Miss Honey took the younger students off on exploration walks. She had many books about wild flowers and plants, but in the November wind, it would be hard to find any of the dried flowers from summer.

"Look for the leaves," Miss Honey called out. "You might be able to identify the flowers from the dried leaves."

Elizabeth started a sketchbook where she drew many of the plants and then identified them and wrote some characteristics. Drawing did not come easily to Elizabeth, but Miss Honey was a very good artist and gave her some pointers about drawing plants. Harry wanted to pick things and give them to Miss Honey, but this day he did not find much that was pretty.

"What about these?" asked Harry, looking at some parsley still a bit green in the herb garden. He picked a sprig and brought it to Miss Honey.

"Thanks, Harry. We could ask Mother if she needs any herbs picked and dried before winter."

"Yeah," said Harry.

Thomas and Sam were not too interested. They hid and then jumped out to scare the others. Each time, Miss Honey always pretended to be terrified and called them "the pirates." Thomas was Terrible Tom Tankard and Sam was Surly Sam Snicker.

"Avast, Matey," said Thomas to Harry, "Give me that there parsley or I will kidnap you and hold you for ransom."

"I'm not 'fraid of you, not when Miss Honey is around," said Harry.

"Don't get lost boys," Miss Honey yelled as the pirates ran down the path to the beach.

The days went on in an autumn that was a bit milder than usual, but always windy. Papa and Mr. Guptil could get ahead on some of the winter chores, and the everyday tasks of drying clothes, keeping warm, and finding food were all rather easy, compared to weeks that were stormy and cold.

One evening after supper Mother said, "Okay, Harry, let's get the dinner dishes done. Then we can have a rest and read a story." Most days now Mother fell asleep during rest time and was awakened by Harry.

"Mother, it's time to go out again and play before dark. Can I go? Can I go see if Freddy Guptil can come out too?"

Freddy was a year younger than Harry, but he wasn't often allowed out to play without his mother watching. The two boys too often got into some kind of mischief. But it was during this time that Mother could sit down for a few moments and compose a letter or darn some socks or do some other quiet chore. Often, when Elizabeth came down from the schoolroom in the afternoon, Mother was still sitting in the big chair in the living room. Sometimes her eyes would be closed. Sometimes she would be in the kitchen starting to prepare supper. Certainly, she would never take a nap. Only Harry napped.

After noticing Mother's pattern for several days, Elizabeth went in, sat beside her, and asked, "Are you feeling all right?"

"I am just fine, Lizzie," she answered, "Just a little tired."

This didn't make much sense to Elizabeth, as life of late had been peaceful for everyone.

"Why are you tired, Mother?" she asked. "It has been so lovely here on Jib for this week."

"Maybe it's the lovely, fresh air, Lizzie," Mother said, not looking straight at Elizabeth.

Elizabeth gave her mother a long hug. "I hope you'll start to have more energy soon. At least before the bad weather comes and there's even more work to do."

"Thank you, Lizzie. I do, too," said Mother quietly.

Later on that evening, while Miss Honey was reading from *Kidnapped*, Elizabeth watched her mother's eyes close. She watched her father looking at her mother. *Something is not right*, she thought to herself. *Something is just not right.*

After reading time, all the children hugged and kissed their parents and went up to bed.

"Tomorrow, Miss Honey is going to help me make words from my letter cards, Lizzie. Pretty soon I will be able to read like you and Thomas and Francis. Pretty soon, Lizzie, really, really!"

"Will you tuck Harry in tonight, Lizzie?" asked Papa.

"Of course," replied Elizabeth.

"But I want Mother," said Harry.

"Not tonight, my boy. I want to talk with Mother for a bit, so you be a good lad and go with Elizabeth."

Harry pouted, but took Elizabeth's hand and she led him upstairs. Elizabeth only half-listened to Harry's bedtime prattle as she helped him into his nightshirt, she thought about her mother. She listened to Harry say his prayers.

> *Now I lay me down to sleep,*
> *I pray the Lord my soul to keep.*
> *When in the morning light I wake,*
> *Help me the paths of love to take.*

"God bless Mother and Papa and Miss Honey and Lizzie and Thomas and Francis and ME! Amen."

"You forgot Nana," said Elizabeth.

"And 'course, Nana. Amen."

Lizzie tickled his stomach and said, "Sleep tight—Don't let the bedbugs bite."

She took her lamp and went out into the hall and started for her room. She could hear her parents and Miss Honey in conversation downstairs. She put the lamp down at the top of the stairs and crept down a few stairs where she could peek around the corner and see a bit, as well as hear the conversation.

"I think we must tell the children soon, Hildy. And you must go to Mary Alice and Archie very soon, as the doctor has prescribed. You mustn't push yourself any longer," said Papa.

"I'd like to stay until Christmas, Will. I am certain I can manage that."

"I can help with the house, Mr. Barton. And I've called the school's office. They are willing to allow me to stay longer than planned. I do have to move on a couple weeks after Thanksgiving, though."

"We can manage." Will Barton looked at his wife. "But, Hildy, you must change your habits right away. We'll tell the children at breakfast that you'll be going to the mainland after Christmas until the child is born. You will need to stay off your feet for the entire afternoon, every day."

"I'll move the children's afternoon lessons to the kitchen, Mrs. Barton. We will clean up after dinner and they can do their work at the kitchen table while I make supper. We might even have some very interesting lessons in the kitchen!"

Hildy Barton reached out to Miss Honey. "Anna, you are so good and clever with the children. We can't thank you enough for your kindnesses to us and to them."

"I'm glad to be able to help you, Mrs. Barton. You have lovely children, and I am so fond of them. If my own children are much like yours, I will be a very happy woman." Mother and Miss Honey embraced each other silently.

Father broke the quietness of the moment, "Well, I say, we must be off to bed. The sun comes up early!"

Elizabeth scampered to her room, still in shock from what she had heard. *Another baby! No! It was not possible! Mother had almost died when Harry was born. We do not need another baby in this family.* Elizabeth's head was on fire with fury.

She flung herself on her bed and pounded her fists and pushed her face into her pillow and screamed. *Why would her parents want another baby? Weren't the four children enough to take care of? Mother will be even sicker with this baby. How would they ever manage if they lost Mother?*

Elizabeth could not console herself. She had no answers to her questions. She could not control the anger that welled up in her chest. *Why? Why? Why?*

The tears streamed down her cheeks and were absorbed by her pillowcase. Her hair was damp on her neck from perspiration. In the jumble of bedcovers, she cried for what seemed hours and then fell asleep in exhaustion, her arms and legs twisted and knotted in her sheets.

Her dreams were not peaceful ones. Mother was flying away to heaven and she was gripping Mother's arm with both of her hands. Finally, she could hold on no longer and Mother floated away.

CHAPTER SEVEN

A Plan

The new morning brought the first rain that Jib had experienced in over a week. Elizabeth woke up with a pounding in her head and her hands clenching the corners of her pillow. She tried to convince herself that what she had heard the night before had been a dream, but she knew that it was not. She had heard the awful news. How would she manage the explanations Papa would give this morning? She looked in the mirror. Her brown eyes were red and swollen and her face was streaked with dried tears. She poured some water from the pitcher into the washbasin and splashed her face, then dried it with her towel and saw little improvement.

After a good brushing, her hair was neat again and tied at her neck in a ribbon. She put on her stockings and bloomers, undershirt and blouse, and then her jumper. She laced up her shoes, tied them, and again looked in the small mirror that hung over her bureau. It was certainly an improvement on the bedraggled creature that had stood in front of it ten minutes earlier. She left her room and went down the stairs to the kitchen.

Mother was taking oatmeal off the stove and Papa was still at the table, which was unusual. He sat drinking his coffee and reading a book. He would usually have had his breakfast much earlier and been outside at the light tower by the time the children had their breakfast. If he was sitting at the table when the children came down for breakfast, they knew there was business to discuss.

"Good morning, Lizzie," Papa said without looking up.

"Good morning," answered Elizabeth, barely audible.

Thomas was gobbling down his porridge, and Francis and Harry came into the kitchen right behind Elizabeth.

"I can't find my boots," said Harry. "Where did I take them off, Lizzie?"

"Look under the table, Harry. I bet you kicked them off during the story last night," answered Elizabeth.

Harry stuck his head under the table. "Yup, you're right," he said as he tugged the black rubber boots on by pulling the sturdy handles. Elizabeth bent down to give them one final pull.

Father put down his book and cleared his throat.

"Mother and I need to discuss something with you children," he began.

Elizabeth gripped the sides of her chair.

Mother and Papa exchanged glances and then Papa began. "Right after Christmas, Mother will be going to the mainland to stay with Mary Alice and Archie Brown until the end of March or early April, when we expect a new child will be born into our family."

The children were silent. Elizabeth stared at the table. Harry, after he closed his gaping mouth, was the only one to speak, but, as luck would have it, he spoke for all the children.

"A baby? A baby? We don't want a baby. I'm the baby here."

Father could not conceal his amusement at Harry's honest expressions.

"Yes, you are right now, Harry, but you are getting too big to be a baby, and Mother and I are very happy that the good Lord has seen fit to bless this family with a new little one for all of us to enjoy." He looked at Elizabeth, who was usually his ally. "What do you think, Lizzie?"

Elizabeth looked at her mother and her father and tears started to flow down her cheeks.

"I'm sorry if the good Lord thought it was a good idea. I think this is a dumb idea. Harry's right. We do not need another baby, especially if it is another boy!" she yelled as she ran from the table.

Her mother got up from the table and followed Elizabeth outside, grabbing two jackets as she went out. She put on one jacket as she caught up to Elizabeth, who was already past the garden.

"Wait, Lizzie. Listen to me." As she reached Elizabeth, who was looking out at the ocean, Mother put the other jacket over Elizabeth's head and shoulders. The pounding of the sea against the cliffs was not as loud as the pounding in Elizabeth's chest. Mother put her arms around Elizabeth from behind and talked calmly into her ear.

"I know it seems as if we are perfect as we are, Lizzie, but try to think of it this way. We would've had five children with Jenny. Maybe this is God's way of giving Jenny back to us." Elizabeth was silent. "Maybe it'll be a sister for you and then you'll have a very special person in your life. I know you're upset about this, but don't decide right now that you don't want this child. How could you not want such a gift as this? You need to give the idea some time, Lizzie. Give it all some time."

Elizabeth turned around and hugged her mother.

"What if you die, Mother? What if you die like you almost did with Harry? What if you leave us all alone? How could we bear to be without you?"

"That's why I am going to the Brown's, dear. They'll be very strict with me and keep me from doing anything I shouldn't. I won't be seeing all the things I should be doing here, so I'll be more apt to do as I'm told and stay in bed, so that everything will go well. The doctor is so close to Archie and Mary Alice that I will be in good hands. It's a good plan, Elizabeth; it is, and I'm counting on your help here on Jib while I'm gone. You'll have to do much more, my big girl. I'm counting on you."

"I know I will, Mother. But I'm really not big enough yet to do all of your work. I want to do my schoolwork, too. I want to pass the exam. Oh, it will be such an awful time." Elizabeth held onto her mother and cried and cried. When her crying turned to sobs and she gradually quieted, Mother wiped her face with her apron and guided her back into the house. Papa had gone out to the light and the boys had gone up to the schoolroom. Elizabeth helped her mother tidy up from breakfast in silence.

"Lizzie, you go along to school, dear. I'll finish here." Mother gave her a squeeze. "Try not to worry, child. I'm not. I know it will be hard, but I'll make certain that Papa has the boys help you all the time. You know he'll make them do their part. And you can call me at the Brown's house when you need help. We can talk every week when I am away. I'm feeling much better now, I'm very excited about the baby, and I have great faith that all will be well. We'll have Miss Honey for a bit longer too. Won't that be fun?" Mother was convincing, but Elizabeth was unconvinced.

In the schoolroom that day the mood was gloomy. Not only had a rainstorm come up, but also the morning news had dampened the spirits of the children. Miss Honey tried to lighten things up by having a singing lesson. The children's voices could barely be heard.

"I've been workin' on the railroad, all the live long day. I've been workin' on the railroad, just to pass the time away. Don't ya hear the whistle blowin'? Rise up so early in the morn. Don't ya hear the captain shoutin,' Dinah, blow your horn!" sang Miss Honey.

"Come on now, help me with the chorus."

Sam Guptil shouted his loudest as he and Thomas usually did when they got to this part, but he was the only one.

"Dinah, won't ya blow, Dinah, won't ya blow, Dinah, won't ya blow your horn, your horn? Dinah, won't ya blow, Dinah, won't ya blow, Dinah, won't ya blow your horn? Someone's in the kitchen with Dinah ..."

Their hearts just weren't in the singing. But Miss Honey did not give up on trying to distract them. There was a spelling bee and a longer-than-usual nature walk, in spite of the rain. Elizabeth asked her if she could have some time to write to her grandmother, and Miss Honey agreed. Elizabeth had thought all day about talking to Nana and wished that Nana were here on Jib with her right now. She thought about it for a few minutes and then wrote:

> Dear Nana,
> I must tell you the awful news we have. Mother is going to have another baby. She is going to have to leave right after Christmas and go to the Brown's and stay until the baby is born. I am worried that she will die, Nana. She was sick when Harry was born, and she almost died. I know you remember. What would we do without Mother? I could not bear it. Why did the good Lord want to give us another

baby? We have enough to do without another baby. It is hard just to have Harry, even if he is getting bigger and easier than before.

I know winter is too hard for you on Jib, but couldn't you please come for a little while? Couldn't you come for Thanksgiving and stay until Christmas and then get off to the mainland the first good day after Christmas? If you will come, I will help you all the time and I will do everything you ask me to do. By Christmas, you will have taught me more than I know now and I will be able to manage until March without you. Please, come. Please.

Your loving granddaughter,

Elizabeth

Elizabeth asked Miss Honey to post her letter when she went over to the mainland on her day off, which happened to be the next day. Dinnertime came and went quietly, though Papa and Mother tried to make some conversation, helped along by Miss Honey.

"Mr. Guptil will take the early evening shift tonight. How about a checkers tournament after dinner, Francis?" asked Papa.

"Okay," replied Francis.

"Can I play, too, Papa, can I?" added Harry.

"You play Thomas or Lizzie, and then whoever wins will play the winner of our game. What do you say, Lizzie?" continued Papa.

"No, thanks, Papa, I am reading a good book just now," replied Lizzie, who normally would have been doing cartwheels all over the house for a checkers tournament, because she loved to beat Papa or Francis. Either one would do.

"I'll play Harry," said Miss Honey. Harry's eyes and mouth got big and wide.

Lizzie felt very small then, as she realized that Miss Honey had done what she should have done. She should have tried to go along with the plan and allowed herself to be cheered up, but she didn't feel up to it. After supper, she helped Miss Honey clean up while Papa took Harry to get into his pajamas before the checkers games. Mother sat in the kitchen rocker and quizzed Thomas on his spelling words and Francis went out briefly to check his traps down by the landing.

It turned out to be a splendid tournament. Francis beat Papa, and a seldom-seen look of ecstasy came over his face. Miss Honey beat Harry and, as Miss Honey was a formidable opponent, it was a hard-fought fight for Francis, but in the end, Francis triumphed.

Then Mother looked up from her knitting and said, "I challenge the champion!" Everyone cheered as Mother stood up and moved to the table while Francis lined up the checkers.

Father went over to the cupboard, and as soon as Harry saw him reach for the popcorn, he went running for the popping kettle.

"I got it, Papa. Let's make two batches, Okay?" he shouted.

"Shhhh, Harry, I'm trying to concentrate!" said Francis, sternly.

"Yes, Harry, Francis will need all his concentration to beat the family checkers champion," said Papa as he winked at Mother.

"Now, Will, I didn't want to intimidate Francis. He did so well against you, he might beat me this time."

"Yeah, he might," said Thomas, who was in his big brother's corner.

Harry and Papa measured out the popcorn in the big kettle. Papa scooped a bit of lard in as well, put the kettle on the hottest part of the stove, and soon the corn was sizzling. Papa grabbed the handles of the kettle with potholders and shook it back and forth. The small pops escalated into a loud chorus that banged on the tin lid of the kettle. Harry put his fingers in his ears and licked his lips. Papa poured the hot corn into a big bowl and sprinkled some salt over it.

"Popcorn's ready," shouted Harry.

"SHHH," yelled Elizabeth, "they are trying to concentrate."

Harry and Papa gobbled the popcorn without competition.

It was a close game, and in the end they were down to two kings for Francis and one for Mother. She was outnumbered and cornered when Francis made a fatal mistake. Mother jumped one of his kings, leaving him with one. Francis glowered at the table. Shortly after, Mother had his last king cornered and took the game.

Francis was a good sport and gave his mother a smile. "You really are the family champion, Mother. But I'll beat you one of these days."

"Of course you will. That's why I'm hanging on to the championship until the last possible moment!" replied Mother.

Miss Honey led Harry upstairs to bed. He was full of popcorn and quite content. Elizabeth went up quietly, after kissing each of her parents. After she was in bed, her father came into her room.

"Goodnight, my favorite daughter," he said, as she threw her arms around his neck and hugged him.

"Goodnight, Papa," she said.

"You know, Lizzie, there is plenty of love in this family for another child. We won't run out of love, ever. Have you learned the word 'infinite' in mathematics yet? Well, infinite means never ending, and love is something that never ends. The more love you give away, the more you have to give. Mother and I have more than enough love for all of you. And we are going to keep Mother as safe as possible so she comes back to us with our new baby. Have some faith, Lizzie, and pray for Mother every night."

"I'll try, Papa. What happens when we die? Do we still give love to our family when we die?"

"Love doesn't ever disappear, Lizzie. We have inside us all the love that was ever given to us by someone who isn't here with us anymore. My father was a sea captain and drowned at sea, as you know. Often when I'm in the light on a stormy night, I feel him there with me, and when I look through the glass, sometimes I think I see his reflection. 'Course, it's really my imagination. But knowing that he loved me so much when he was here on earth keeps me comforted."

Lizzie hugged her father and he hugged her in return. She went off to sleep with the ease of a newborn.

CHAPTER EIGHT

Papa's Surprise

November continued to be a splendid but cold month. On the clear days in October, the multicolored hills on the mainland had been easy to see, and Lizzie had watched them turn from green to yellow and orange and red and finally to brown, as the leaves dropped to the ground and left the branches bare. Without leaves, the mainland looked like a different place altogether. More houses and other buildings stood out along the shoreline.

She often used Papa's binoculars to study the coastline. She could see the entire church, instead of just the steeple. She could see the school and longed to be a part of the groups of girls she imagined playing in the schoolyard. The roads along the shoreline were busy with cars and trucks moving here and there, some of them heading for the great cities of the East Coast where Elizabeth yearned to go and explore. She stood often at the schoolroom window, watching through the binoculars for any activity she found on the mainland.

Once, she saw a group of children romping on the wharf. It looked like a game of tag. *Oh, how lovely it would be to have enough children for a good game of tag.* She did play with Thomas and Harry and the Guptil boys. But a large group, with other girls, would be ideal, she thought.

Soon the chill of late November was in the air. Lizzie's hands felt icy as she brought in the clothes that were slightly frozen on the clothesline. The clothespins fought with her when she tried to remove them. There was no question that winter was coming. During the first week of November the weather was crisp and cold, but not stormy. As the second week began, the winds whipped the sea into a tempest.

Father and Mr. Guptil had repaired the wooden winter walk-ways and the knotted ropes, which adults and children gripped when they walked to the light, between houses, or to the storage areas. For the most part, though, Elizabeth and her younger brothers had to stay in the house.

Sometimes Harry was bundled up to go visit the Guptil boys at their house. Sometimes Elizabeth would beg to be allowed to take some coffee out to Papa at the light. She didn't mind the fierce wind biting her nose and cheeks and she didn't mind the rain, as rough as sandpaper on her hands. It made her body feel good and clean after so many days in the house.

After a three-day blow of strong, northeast winds, Elizabeth saw patches of blue in the seaward sky when she awoke in the morning. She dressed quickly and went down to breakfast. Mother was in the kitchen sitting in her rocker with a sleepy Harry, and Miss Honey was pouring some coffee and fixing a biscuit for Mother.

"Good morning, Mother. Good morning, Miss Honey," Elizabeth said exuberantly.

"Good morning, dear," said Mother, as Elizabeth hugged her mother's neck and ruffled Harry's hair.

"Good morning, Elizabeth," replied Miss Honey. "Maybe we can take a nature walk after dinner today, if the weather breaks. I think we all need to stretch our legs."

"I was hoping that you would say that," replied Elizabeth.

Papa came into the kitchen from his work. He went to the stove, poured himself a cup of coffee, and sat down in his chair at the table. "The seas seem to be calming considerably," he said. "I think we can get to the mainland today and get the supplies that have been waiting on the dock for us. We'll launch the boat after dinner."

"Oh, Papa!" exclaimed Elizabeth. "May I go, Papa, please, may I go?" she pleaded.

Papa glanced at Mother and then back at Elizabeth, and back to Mother again. "Do you need anything in town, Hildy?" he asked.

"Actually, I have a small list, and if Elizabeth could go to the store and get these things, we'd be sure to have them, even if the weather turns on us again soon. You never know when you'll get the chance to go ashore again, Will."

Elizabeth held her breath while she awaited Papa's answer.

"Guess that's a good plan, then, Hildy," he replied, almost drowned out by Elizabeth's whoops of delight.

"What about me?" yelled Harry, but no one paid much attention to him.

"All right, young lady, calm down. There's no room in my boat for a wild hyena," said Papa, attempting to be stern.

"Elizabeth," said Miss Honey, "I have a small list, as well. Would you get a few things for me at the store?"

"Of course, of course," Elizabeth replied, as she hopped gently around the kitchen.

"What about me?" asked Harry again.

Thomas came in during the last bit of the excitement and entreated his father to take him, too. "I can help Lizzie with the carrying if you let me come, Papa."

"Would you be a help to Lizzie, and mind her, Tom?" Papa asked.

"Yup, I'll do whatever she says," Thomas replied.

Elizabeth quietly rolled her eyes at Miss Honey. She knew that if she complained about Thomas's coming, she mightn't be allowed to go either.

"All righty, then," said Papa, "Two to town it is. We'll go after dinner. Now, work hard on your lessons this morning you two." He winked at Miss Honey.

"What about me?" said Harry, much louder.

"Not this time, boy," said Papa, patting Harry's head. "Your mother needs you to stay with her today." Harry's hopeful face fell, but he knew Papa wouldn't change his mind.

Elizabeth and Thomas gobbled their porridge, finished their chores in a flash, and nearly flew up to the classroom ahead of Miss Honey.

It seemed to be a very long morning to both Thomas and Elizabeth. Harry pouted to Miss Honey as he came in for his lesson.

"I think we'll give Sam and Francis a holiday from their lessons this afternoon, too, and you and I will go out to find some bayberry and juniper for the Thanksgiving decorations. What do you think, Harry?" she asked.

She couldn't have pleased him more if she'd given him a huge candy bar and told him he didn't have to share it.

The conversation at dinner was full of instructions and directions for the trip to town.

"Mr. Wallace at the store has some shoelaces put aside for me. Now, look at the thread he has and see if you can match this piece of fabric for a dress I'm making. Get it a tad bit lighter than the fabric rather than darker, if you can. We also need a new supply of baking powder. Check and make sure the can is sealed. The last can we had lost its zip far too soon. He's supposed to have a bushel of carrots and one of squash." Mother continued giving Elizabeth her list for the store and told Thomas several times to do what Elizabeth asked without complaint.

"Mother, may I take a nickel from my bank to buy some penny candy?" asked Thomas.

"Yes, you both may, and here is a dime to buy some for Harry and Francis, as well."

"Papa, would you buy some Necco wafers, please?" asked Harry. "We can all share them."

Right after eating, Thomas and Elizabeth found their warmest coats, retrieved their hats and mittens, and laced up their boots. They kissed Mother goodbye and ran down to the boat being readied by Papa and Mr. Guptil.

Launching the boat was always tricky in these waters, and today was no exception. As usual, Papa started the engine once before the boat was in the water to make certain that it would start. As soon as it hit water, he started it again and steered quickly away from the shore.

Elizabeth and Thomas climbed aboard and sat in the middle of the boat and Mr. Guptil sat in the bow, as it was lowered over the water. Papa went through his routine, but the engine did not start as expected. He tried again as the boat moved closer to the water and the rocks. Elizabeth could see the seaweed hanging from the rocks and thought she could reach out and touch it. When it looked like they might crash any second, the engine sputtered and caught and Papa swung the boat out and away from the rocks.

The children sighed and looked at their father. They were in awe of his skill and of their good fortune. Francis was watching from the cliff, where even he gave a slight wave of his hand, recognizing that they had all been spared from disaster. Then, all eyes were on the mainland and the day's adventure continued.

From a distance, Elizabeth saw a puff of smoke near the shoreline as the afternoon train pulled out of the station on its way through from Portland. Although she felt she should be satisfied with a trip to town, the desire to jump aboard the train was still quite strong.

The sturdy boat pounded some in the rough water, but the white-caps subsided as they entered the harbor, and the boat eased into a space at the dock. Since the tide was on its way out, the children scrambled a long way up the ladder to reach the dock, and then up the ramp to the wharf. Papa and Mr. Guptil tied the boat and joined the children on the wharf.

"Off with you now to your errands," Papa ordered. "We will be leaving in an hour, so be back here on time. We have to reach Jib before supper. It gets dark early."

Elizabeth and Thomas flew to the general store. They were not disappointed when they opened the door. The little bell jingled and wonderful smells greeted them at once. Pickles and cinnamon, kerosene, animal feed, and bread. Whatever made that peculiar and particular store smell overwhelmed them and brought wide smiles to their faces as they entered.

"Good afternoon, little Bartons," said Mrs. Wallace from behind the counter. "How are things out on Jib?"

"Just fine, Mrs. Wallace," answered Elizabeth.

"I 'magine you want the things your mother's been waitin' for," Mrs. Wallace said.

"Yes, ma'am, I do, and a few more things, as well."

Elizabeth set to her task of locating all of Mother's needs right off. She asked to look at the thread colors and chose one she thought was just right. She and Mrs. Wallace went to work getting everything else together.

"Thomas," Elizabeth called to her brother, who had his nose stuck to the penny candy case. "You should carry this basket of squash to the wharf and then come right back for the carrots. It will take several trips to get all of this to the boat. Thomas rolled his eyes at Elizabeth and then quickly remembered his promise to his mother.

"Sure, Lizzie."

*   *   *   *

Thomas lifted the basket and carried it out the shop door and down the steps to the street. It was heavy and it took him a while to get to the wharf, because he had to put it down every now and again. It was on one of these stops that Thomas noticed a woman walking toward the wharf carrying a small bag. A young man was with her carrying a suitcase. Thomas could not believe his eyes.

"Nana?" he thought. "NANA!" he cried out.

The woman turned and saw Thomas running toward her. Her smile was broad and warm.

"Thomas, what are you doing in town?" she asked.

"Nana, what are you doing in town?" he replied, and they both laughed.

Nana turned to the young man who held her suitcase. "This is my grandson, Thomas Barton, who lives on Jib. It looks like I won't need your services to get me to the island." She reached in her purse and took out some silver coins to pay him. "Thank you very much for your help, young man. I appreciate your willingness."

The young man tipped his cap and headed back toward the railroad station.

"How were you going to get to Jib, Nana?" asked Thomas.

"I was hoping to find one of the fishermen to take me. If I couldn't get there this afternoon, I was going to call from Archie's and have your father come for me in the morning. How wonderful that you are here!"

Thomas was still amazed. "We came over to get supplies after the storm."

"I left after the storm, too, and hoped to get to you before there was another one. What great luck! Who is here with you?"

"Lizzie is still in the store, and Papa is on the wharf."

"You go down to the wharf with your basket, Thomas, and then come back for my bags. Put them on the wharf where Papa won't see them. When you've done that, come to the store. I want to surprise Elizabeth—now don't you tell your Papa! Okay?"

"Okay, Nana. I can't wait to see his face when he sees you coming with Lizzie!"

*   *   *   *

Nana walked over to the store. When she pushed the door open, the bell on the door jingled, but Elizabeth didn't look up. She had finished her shopping and was staring into the window of the candy counter.

"I'll have two sticks of red licorice and two root beer barrels, please, and a roll of Necco wafers too, thank you," she said to Mrs. Wallace.

Elizabeth heard a voice come from behind her.

"I'm not sure this young woman should have any candy at all."

Elizabeth turned quickly, realizing the voice was a familiar one, and saw her grandmother's smile as she teased her very confused granddaughter.

"Nana!" she screamed, throwing her arms around the laughing old woman. "Nana, you came. You came!"

"Yes, I did. Did you think I would let you down? Never! But let's let your letter be our secret. We will just tell your father that I wanted to be here for Thanksgiving and Christmas this year."

"Do you think he would be angry?" Elizabeth whispered.

"I bet he would have wanted you to talk to him before you went calling on me. His feelings could be a mite hurt, if you know what I mean," replied her grandmother.

"I … I guess I do. I'm sorry, Nana."

"Now don't go being sorry. I don't need a reason to come back up here to see you, now do I? Even if I only left two weeks ago. We won't tell anyone exactly the reason, will we?"

"Nope," replied Elizabeth, with a chuckle.

Just then, Thomas returned.

"Goodbye, Mrs. Wallace," they all called as they carried the last of the packages out of the store and headed to the wharf.

In the distance, they could see their father waiting with his hands on his hips. As they got closer, they watched the expression on his face change from annoyance to surprise. Then his mouth dropped open a bit and the children began to laugh.

"Hello, Willie," Nana yelled. She was the only one who called him Willie.

"Mother, what are you doing here?" he asked.

"I was going to ask you the same thing. I expected to hire a fisherman to take me out to Jib, and here you were waiting for me. How kind of you. Who told you I was coming?" Nana replied.

"No one! Why are you here?" he asked.

"Do I have to wait for an invitation to spend the holidays with my children and grandchildren?" she asked.

"No, 'course not," replied Papa, and that was the end of the discussion.

CHAPTER NINE

Harry

"Harry, go see if Papa's boat is coming. It's about time." Harry ran to the window in the living room that faced the mainland.

"I do see the boat, Mother. It's coming, and it's almost here. I can see Papa and Thomas and Lizzie, and I can see Nana, too!"

"Now, Harry, you have too much imagination today. You can't be seeing Nana," said Mother.

"Yes, I do see Nana. It's not my 'magination. I do. I do." Miss Honey and Mother looked at each other. Miss Honey left the kitchen and joined Harry at the window. "See, there's Nana, right next to Lizzie."

"Well, there is another person there, Mrs. Barton," called Miss Honey, "in a black coat and hat."

Mother ran to the window and picked up the spyglass. She couldn't believe what she saw, but it was indeed Nana. "Well, I'll be, here she is just when I need her," Mother said softly.

Mother threw on her coat and walked down toward the boathouse followed by Miss Honey, as Mr. Guptil and Thomas helped Nana out of the boat and onto the walkway. Elizabeth took Nana's arm and brought her to where Mother was standing.

Mother reached out her arms and hugged and hugged Nana with all her might. "Oh, I can't believe you've come just when I need you most of all."

Miss Honey chimed in, "I'm so glad I'll get to know the 'Nana' the children have spoken about so fondly."

Even Francis gave his grandmother a hug and grinned from ear to ear. He loved Nana's famous brown sugar fudge and knew she would make some!

Harry shouted while swinging on the porch railing, "Nana, I know all my letters and I go to school. I do, don't I, Miss Honey? I do!"

"I'll bet you are the smartest one, Harry. I'll just bet," Nana said.

"I am. I really am," he replied, blinking his wide, blue eyes.

Nana touched the top of Harry's head, "Your father had the same determination and the same wide, blue eyes, too."

Elizabeth put her mother's packages on the table in the kitchen and ran up to her room to get it ready for Nana. Her bed would be much warmer tonight and she would get a song before she went to sleep, but only after saying her prayers.

Such a luxury to have Nana here for the holidays. Such a luxury. I hope Mother and Papa won't find out that I am the reason for Nana's coming back to Jib. I think they might be angry if they knew I wrote the letter to her, begging her to come..

Supper was delightful, with everyone scrambling to talk at once and fill Nana in on all the events. Even Francis gave a running inventory of the wildfowl shot and eaten and the number of lobsters he had caught since she had left. Thomas recounted the day of inspection and let Nana know that Jib was a top-notch light station.

"And the inspector even said that Papa is one of the best, and we are all excellent helpers," he said proudly.

"Well now, Thomas," said Papa.

"He did; you heard him," insisted Thomas.

"Yup," said Harry, "The guv'ment said we were the best, and Mother was sick and we did all the work and everything."

"Hildy, you're never sick," Nana said. "What was wrong? Are you feeling okay now?" Elizabeth could tell that Nana had been looking for an entrance into the subject of Mother's health, and Harry gave her one as big as a barn door, and then he gave all the answers, too.

"Mother's going to have a baby, Nana. Didn't you know that? And I want another brother so I can be the big brother to a boy, and Lizzie wants a sister, and Mother is going to the mainland to wait for my brother to come. She's goin' right after Christmas, and I have to be good for Lizzie, right Papa?"

Lizzie kicked Harry under the table. The room was silent until Papa spoke. "We hadn't gotten around to tellin' you, but we would have soon enough. But, yes, there'll be one more come spring."

"Well, well. I guess we have some work to do and I don't mean just for the holidays. Nana looked around the table and saw that no one seemed very happy, except for Harry, who did not understand their concern. So Nana took a deep breath and spoke the words she had rehearsed to herself on the train.

"You know, children, a new life is the greatest work of God. When each of you was brand new, we were delighted to have you. You were special gifts to us. We watched you carefully and cheered as you did each new thing, from your first smile to your first step to your first word. It would be a sad thing if this new baby weren't welcomed into the Barton family the same way. There will always be enough for each of you, too. Enough food and enough love. We need to all work together to get ready for this wonderful event. I suggest that you add to the things you plan to do for Christmas one small thing for your new brother or sister."

"Brother!" said Harry.

"Sister!" said Elizabeth, louder than Harry.

"Now, now," said Papa, relieved at the break in the tension, "We'll have none of that!"

"I think that's a good idea, Nana," said Mother.

"Who wants to help me make a quilt for Baby Barton, then?"

"I'd love to help!" replied Miss Honey.

"I can cut out pieces now, Nana," added Harry. "I'm 'lowed to use the scissors if someone is with me."

Nana looked at Elizabeth. "And can you help me, Lizzie?" she asked.

"I guess so. How about using that pink material left over from my quilt?" she asked with a sly grin.

Afternoon brought the sense of peace and comfort that usually prevailed when Nana was with them. Harry was put to work cutting out squares of fabric at the kitchen table. Mother was able to take a good nap in her chair, while Nana and Miss Honey and Elizabeth did the cleaning up in a quarter of the time it would take Elizabeth by herself.

After supper, they gathered in the living room to hear Miss Honey read the next chapter of *Kidnapped*. Thomas was lying on his back on the braided rug and Harry was sitting on Miss Honey's lap. Francis was carving some wood with his jackknife, while Mother and Papa were relaxed in their chairs and Elizabeth sat on the floor with her head in her grandmother's lap.

"Stay tuned for the next chapter, tomorrow night," said Miss Honey when she finished.

By this time Harry was asleep and had slid to the floor. Papa reached down, scooped him up, and headed off up the stairs with him. Thomas thanked Miss Honey, Francis gave her a nod, and Elizabeth put her finger to her mouth.

"Shhh," she said, pointing to Nana's nodding head. They all giggled, and that woke Nana from her little nap.

"Oh! It must be time for bed," said Nana, as the giggles turned to loud roars and the children tumbled over each other on the living room rug, stopping only to gasp for short breaths. Nana and Mother let them tire themselves out and then looked at each other and nodded. "Time for bed," they said together.

"No, not yet," cried Thomas, as Papa, who had returned to the living room, picked him up and carried him toward the stairs. Elizabeth trailed along behind, still giggling, and Nana, with a large grin, watched them disappear up the stairs.

CHAPTER TEN

The Holidays

The days that followed Nana's return to Jib Island were full of busy hours. The daily indoor chores of mealtimes, laundry, schoolwork, and cleaning and, in addition, the lightkeeping chores outside at the lighthouse, were enough to keep the family active all day. Before Christmas everyone was busy with little projects. Hiding these treasures and trying to keep them hidden became a great game for all of them.

Nana had uncovered the Singer sewing machine in the corner of the living room and the "quilting group" was busy making a quilt for the new baby.

"I have ten more squares, Nana," said Harry, as he ran to the sewing corner. "You have all the other ones put together yet?" he asked.

"Slow down, Harry, I can't keep up," she replied.

"Let me see. How big is it now?" he pestered. "Wow, that's pretty good, Nana. It's getting bigger. I like the pinwheels. How do you do that?"

Nana smiled at Harry's endless questions. "Well, I take the squares that you cut and I cut 'em again, so they are triangles. Then I sew 'em back together with two different colors to each square. Here … look. Can you put 'em together to look like pinwheels? That's right. It's just like a puzzle, isn't it?"

"Yup, a puzzle. Then you take the pinwheel squares and put more and more together and it gets bigger and bigger."

"Right, and then I add some rectangles—long ones and short ones—and pretty soon the quilt top will be finished."

Harry watched his grandmother sew the quilt top for a while and then he went back to the kitchen. "Nana and I have the quilt top almost done," he announced to no one in particular.

"That's good, Harry. Wash up for dinner," said Mother. "And you can ring the bell."

Elizabeth was finishing the table setting when everyone started coming in to dinner. Francis was the first one in, as he was most often the hungriest. It was Thomas's turn to say grace.

"Bless this food which now we take, and do us good for heaven's sake. Amen."

"Amen," they all echoed.

"Francis," said Papa, "what kind of bird do you think you can get us for Thanksgiving?"

Francis was slow to answer. "Well, Pa, I thought if you could take me up to that mountainside behind the blueberry fields, I might be able to get something better than what I can get here on Jib."

"Now, I suspected you might want a hunting trip before the holiday and I guess we could go, if we get a good day."

"Thomas could come, too, Pa. He's getting to be a pretty good shot."

Thomas sat tall and puffed out his chest. "Can I come, Pa, can I?"

"I don't see why not, if we get a good day."

The boys exchanged proud glances. Thomas tried to stay calm like Francis.

When Francis finished his dinner, he took a piece of wood out of his pocket, flipped open his jackknife and began to work.

"What are you making, Francis?" asked Elizabeth.

"That's for you to guess," he answered.

Elizabeth watched him for a few minutes, but couldn't figure out what he was carving.

The days passed with only four remaining until Thanksgiving, but the hunting trip was put off as the seas were rough and the winds were high. The sky was becoming a winter gray-blue and the days shorter and shorter. The afternoon darkness, with streaks of charcoal-colored clouds passing through, was a sure sign of winter weather ahead. When Harry wanted to play at the Guptils', he had to be walked over to their house by someone bigger and heavier. The wind was strong enough to lift him up and blow him away out to sea.

Nana, Mother, Elizabeth, and Miss Honey stayed inside for the most part. The quilt top was finished and they began to quilt it together.

The quilt top had been pieced by sewing all the small shapes together to make a pattern of pinwheels. The finished quilt top was layered with an old blanket in the middle and a piece of solid color cotton on the back. With sturdy thread and a strong needle, they put ties on the squares from the quilt top through all the layers and up to the top again where they tied a strong knot and cut the ends leaving an inch of thread. These ties held the pieces from shifting out of place. Then small stitches with a fine thread were sewn in to make a pattern. The result was a sturdy, warm and beautiful quilt.

Two days before Thanksgiving, Papa woke Thomas and Francis just before dawn. "I believe we have a chance to go today," he said. "Get dressed and be quick."

Thomas and Francis moved as if they had been shot from a slingshot. They dressed and came to the kitchen in minutes. Papa had the porridge made and they wolfed it down in great gulps, threw on their warm clothes, grabbed their guns and followed Papa out the door. The early light was just enough for them to make out a clear sky. The wind was soft and the few small trees toward the center of the island were motionless shadows. They lowered the boat and started the engine. It responded with a kick and a whir, and away they went toward the mainland.

As soon as the boys and Papa were out of the house, Nana began to awaken Elizabeth. "C'mon now. Let's get goin.'"

Elizabeth pulled on her clothes quickly and went to wake up Miss Honey and Mother. "They're gone," she said. "Let's get started." By the time everyone assembled in the kitchen, Nana had the coffee on and the porridge cooking. She had put out on the table a finished quilt top. Needles and quilting thread were laid out on the cloth and the needles were threaded. As soon as they had some porridge, Nana gave directions.

"I've marked in the design and it is all pinned to keep it straight, so let's start."

"How did you get this ready by yourself?" asked Elizabeth.

"Well, now, I have to tell the truth. Miss Honey helped me up in the schoolroom one night. It is such a long quilt; it was difficult to put together. You are right, Elizabeth, you always need two to pull things straight and get all the batting smooth between the top and the back." She patted Miss Honey's hand. "Miss Honey is a quick learner."

"It really is beautiful, Daisy!" said Mother.

"Let's go, now. Elizabeth, you work this end. Remember to keep your stitches as small as you can. Four to a needle is what you are aiming to make. Hildy, take the other end, and Anna and I will work the long sides. Anna and I marked all the lines very lightly, so you will have to look carefully to see the design."

They began to work on the pattern of scrolled lines in the bright blue and red border fabric. The white thread showed the lovely lines of the swirls flowing around the quilt, as each set of stitches was completed.

After an hour or so, a sleepy Harry stumbled into the kitchen, still in his pajamas and wrapped in a blanket, his hair a mess of curls scattered helter-skelter over his head.

"Hey, what're you doing? Where's breakfast?"

Mother stopped long enough to get Harry some porridge and sat him in a chair away from the new quilt. He ate quietly. As Harry became more and more awake, he began to look carefully at the quilt. "Hey, that's not the baby's quilt. There's no pink in this. Where'd it come from? What's this quilt for?"

"Now, Harry," said his mother, "this quilt is a big secret. It is a Christmas present. Are you a big enough boy that you can keep a very big secret?"

"Yup, I am BIG and I can keep a BIG secret." His eyes were wide.

"Okay, then. This is a quilt for Francis. He has needed a new one since he grew so tall. Elizabeth got the last one we made, so we thought we would surprise him for Christmas."

"Okay," said Harry, "Won't tell him," stuffing his mouth with the porridge.

"You won't tell anyone, not even Papa. Okay?" said Elizabeth.

"Okay, okay," said Harry, who continued to look carefully at the quilt. "This is a really fun quilt. Look at all the pictures of fish and ducks."

"I found the fabric in Boston last winter," said Nana, "and have been hiding it until we could get to work on the quilt. The plain pieces in between the pictures are from the boys' and Papa's old shirts."

"How come the pieces are all crooked? I cut better than that, Nana!" said Harry.

"You bet you do, but this is a special kind of quilt. It's called a 'crazy quilt.' See, we stitched in some of Francis's ribbons from the agricultural fair and a flannel piece from the wrapping of his first knife. It's really a special quilt just for him. Some people call these 'memory quilts.'"

"How are my stitches, Nana? Small enough? I'm staying on the lines pretty much. Well, here I didn't. Is it ok?" asked Elizabeth.

"Let me see," said Mother. "Hmmm. I think it will do. A few little stitches out of the way won't hurt any quilt. We don't want one that looks like store-bought goods."

"No, we don't," added Nana. "We want Francis to know that we all worked on this and put our best into it. But, like each of us, and him, it's not perfect."

"But, Nana," said Harry. "You said that I'm pretty perfect."

"I guess I did, but that's when you were very little. Now that you are getting bigger, you will get less and less perfect," Nana said, and the others laughed while Harry looked puzzled.

*   *   *   *

The work of preparing for the holidays continued. Francis and Thomas brought home a nice fat Canada goose and a big wild turkey for the Thanksgiving feast. Papa stopped at the general store in Rockland, where he bought cranberries and penny candy. He also brought back a warm woolen shawl for Mother, as it was her birthday the day after Thanksgiving.

"It's beautiful, Will," said Mother, as he wrapped it around her.

"Thangu fr cndy," said Harry, with his mouth full of licorice and his nose stuck right in the little bag to see what else it held. Papa gave Mother a squeeze and thumped Harry gently on the head with his broad knuckles.

"Don't talk with your mouth full, young man," he said, trying not to laugh.

Thanksgiving dinner was an abundant display of foods from the

Jib pantry and the mainland. As was the tradition, the Guptils were invited to join the Bartons. Sam and Freddy and Harry played with blocks in the living room, while Papa and Mr. Guptil talked lighthouse business.

"I'll take the late shift tonight, Will, if you like. Then you can get a full night's sleep," said Roy Guptil.

"Appreciate that, Roy. I must be gettin' old, 'cause that hunting trip really wore me out," replied Papa.

Neither lightkeeper ever got a full-day holiday, as someone had to tend the light—holiday or not. They did take a break from some of the chores before they went back to business as usual, taking turns with the night schedule.

The older children, Miss Honey, and Mrs. Guptil worked under Mother's and Nana's direction until the table was laden with food. The two crispy, well-stuffed birds were in the center, surrounded by potatoes and butternut squash from the summer garden, pickles, green beans, and dandelion greens from the canning pantry, cranberry relish, and even store-bought olives that Mother had been saving.

When all was ready, Mother called them to the table.

"A beautiful sight, Hildy," said Papa.

"It certainly is," added Mr. Guptil. "Sure'r nice looking birds, Francis."

Francis blushed and said a quiet, "Thank you."

"My favorite thing about Thanksgiving is cranberry relish," said Mrs. Guptil, who had made the apple and pumpkin pies for dessert.

"And my favorite is penny candy!" said Harry.

When they were seated, Papa asked everyone to join hands while he said grace.

"We thank thee, heavenly Father, for this amazing table of plenty before us. We are aware of our good fortune and of the thoughtful ways you provide for us with thy bounty. Bless those who are not celebrating this holiday with such splendid gifts as ours. Help us to remember them in our prayers and to do for them by sharing our gifts. Bless each of us, and bless all of us in our lives as families and as friends. Thank you for allowing Nana to be with us this holiday. We also ask you to watch over Mother in these months to come and bring her and the new child safely home to us. Keep us in thy care all the days of our lives. Amen."

"Let's eat!" said Thomas, reaching for the pickles that had been placed in front of him.

*   *   *   *

On Thanksgiving night, the whole family gathered around Miss Honey after she read from *Jo's Boys* and presented her with the gifts they had made for her for Christmas.

"I will take them with me all wrapped, and as I open each one on Christmas, I will think of you," she said. She had tried not to have tears in her eyes, but she couldn't help herself.

The day after Thanksgiving was beautiful, and Miss Honey left Jib to go to the next family. She was being sent to Libby Island to organize studies for the six children in the Philbin family and would spend Christmas with them. Everyone on Jib was sorry to see her go because she had become like a family member. She had taught them their reading and writing and 'rithmetic, and they had taught her about the plants and animals of Jib, how to cook the island menu, and how to make a quilt. Her nightly reading had been a pleasure for all the Barton family and they would miss her.

"Bye now, Francis," said Miss Honey as she gave Francis an adult handshake. "I hope you do well on the tests in the spring. I left you lots of reading and arithmetic assignments, and I expect to be back just before you take the test to have a study session. If anything happens that I can't make it, you know what to do. I know you do."

Francis rolled his eyes. "Yes, Miss Honey. Of course I will do my best," he said with a forced sincerity.

Miss Honey could not resist. She threw her arms around him in a great bear hug.

"Don't you shirk your work, hear? I will be checking up on you and there will be consequences for the wicked," she said as she pinched his cheek with a gleeful smile.

"Ouch!" said Francis. "Okay, okay, I will do it."

The children went out to the boat with their mother to say good-bye. As they stood on the rocks with the cold air blowing gently around them, Miss Honey hugged each one, saving the last hug for Harry, who was crying.

"You be good, Harry, and do the work I left for you. When I get back, I bet you'll be reading all by yourself. I will write you a letter and maybe you can read it with Elizabeth to help a little. Oh, don't cry now. Remember, you're a big boy."

"I … know … I … am … a … big … boy, but … I will miss … you too much," Harry sniffed. "When are you coming back?"

"I will probably be back just when your mother comes home with the baby," she answered.

"That's a long time," Harry whimpered.

"It's not really. You have Christmas to look forward to, and after that you mark every day off on the calendar as I showed you."

"Okay, I will. Bye, Miss Honey."

"Bye, Big Harry."

Francis helped her into the boat and Miss Honey waved as they lowered her to the sea. They all watched and waved. The little boat bounced a bit through the waves and soon it was hard to make out the people on the boat. It headed straight to Rockland, where Miss Honey would get the train and be at Libby Island by the next day. Mother, Nana, Elizabeth, Thomas, and Harry all walked slowly back to the house.

The house seemed empty. Elizabeth hung on to her grandmother's arm. "You know, Nana," she said, "this is how I feel when you leave. I have a big pain in my stomach and I just want to go to my room and curl up on my bed."

"I feel the same way, my girl," replied Nana, "every time I leave you." She gave Elizabeth a little squeeze on her arm and a wink of her eye. "Goodbyes don't get any easier when you are old. Sometimes I think they get harder. I think of you and your parents and brothers all the time after I go home. I'm always missing you and wondering what you are doing. It isn't easy to be away from Jib."

No, thought Elizabeth, it probably isn't. But she still wanted to give it a try and travel to all the wonderful places she thought about, and swim in the waters of Barbados.

CHAPTER ELEVEN

Christmas

S ecret preparations for Christmas were ongoing, and the household plans were organized. One evening, after the children had gone to bed, Mother and Nana had a few quiet moments in the living room while they waited for Papa to come in from the light.

"I would love to get to the store just once before Christmas," said Mother.

"Hildy, you know that's not a good idea," replied Nana. "It'd be too risky in these waters and too much of a strain. Bad enough you'll have to make the trip after Christmas to go to the Brown's. I'm glad you can go there. Mary Alice and Arch will be good for you. They'll be firm, but what a wonderful sense of fun they have; they'll keep your spirits up."

"I am lucky to have them," agreed Mother. "Guess I'll just have to send Will with the list this year and let him take the children on the trip. Do you mind staying here with me, Daisy?"

"Not a'tall, dear, don't you worry. Will and the children can handle this just fine. 'Course, they may bring home a few things not on the list! Speakin' of lists, is your Sears and Roebuck order ready yet?"

"Finished it last week and Mr. Guptil took it to the mail when he went to the mainland. That scamp, Thomas, was hanging 'round the table as I fixed the order, trying hard as he could to see what I had written. Fixed him—I wrote some things, and then when he had gone, crossed them out and wrote the real things. He's probably disappointed thinking that he is getting new long underwear," said Mother.

Nana chuckled. "Serves him right for bein' so nosy!"

*   *   *   *

The day for the trip to the mainland arrived according to the weather. They had waited each day for just the proper conditions: no storm, not too much wind. Papa announced the trip as soon as the children came down for breakfast, and they buzzed around like a swarm of bees after new poppies to get their chores done. Everything had to pass the keeper's inspection before they left, and all had to be dressed warmly for the voyage. This year, since Harry was to be included, Nana helped him into his long underwear, woolen knickers and socks, and shirt and sweaters. She put on two layers under his coat and tied his scarf tightly around his head so his knit cap wouldn't blow off.

"Harry!" said Francis, "you look like a blue, woolen snowman!"

"Never you mind, Francis. Just make sure he stays in the boat, or he will sink right to the bottom," reminded Nana.

The bundled group walked to the landing, where they opened the great doors of the boathouse, only to be greeted by a frightening crash of waves shooting up from the cliff through an opening in the wall at the other end. Papa, Francis, and Thomas pushed the stern of the boat and she thrust her great bow in the air as she slid down the slip to the water. Elizabeth held Harry back so he wouldn't get hurt. Once the engine had been tested, the children boarded the boat and began the journey.

The spray spit around them as they took off through the waves. Everyone shivered and gritted their teeth with the wind blowing and whistling around their covered ears. It nipped their skin through every woolen layer. Elizabeth held Harry close to her, trying to shelter him. The morning sun reflected in the ocean prisms and sparkled like fireworks. They squinted against the splashes and the brightness, each water droplet sparkling like acres of mirror bits. But no one complained, as there was no more exciting day in the whole year; it was as exciting as Christmas day.

After mooring the boat and boarding the tender, they rowed to the wharf. They entered the store as quietly as a tidal wave hits an island, dispersing to all parts, searching for their treasure like so many miniature explorers. The usual smells greeted them, and soon they were too warm.

"Fine day, Mr. Barton!" said Mr. Wallace, welcoming them.

"Yes, 'tis. But need to make good use of it and get back to Jib well by one o'clock." replied Papa. "Here's Hildy's order. I'll leave you to get it together while we go out to Browns' for a tree. Francis, see that all you children have your things on the counter before we leave to get the tree. You've a half hour or so to do your shopping while I go down t' the hardware and get a few parts for one of the engines."

"Yes, Pa," replied Francis.

And so, as they looked at all the wonderful things in the store, they also looked at the money they had carefully unwrapped from their pockets. The children began to make their selections, each one going to the counter separately so the others wouldn't see the purchases. Francis was secretive about his choices, as was Thomas, while Elizabeth helped Harry do his shopping.

"Lizzie, help me pick something for Mother," said Harry.

"I'm getting her some Jergens lotion," whispered Elizabeth. "Do you want to give it to her with me? We can put our money together and get the big bottle, or you can get her some powder to go with it. Here's some that smells like lavender."

"Lemme smell," said Harry. "Mmmm, I like that. Do I have enough money?"

"Show me what you have," said Elizabeth, looking into Harry's little fist, which was clenched around some coins. "Five, ten, eleven, twelve, thirteen, fourteen … yup, you do."

Pretty soon Papa was back. "All set, Bartons?" he called.

"Just a minute more," called Thomas, the last one at the counter.

They set their things aside to be picked up on their way back and went outside to meet Papa. As this was a normal winter in Maine, the roads were covered with a combination of potholes and icy bumps that made driving unsafe and could damage the car. Papa's car was always stored in the Browns' barn. He never took it out in the winter. As a result, they set out on foot to find and cut their tree.

"Jingle bells, jingle bells, jingle all the way," sang Elizabeth.

"Oh, what fun it would be if we just had a sleigh-ay!" added Thomas, as Francis chased him up the road with a handful of snow, threatening to stuff it down his coat. Harry practiced skipping, his newfound skill, and Elizabeth twirled in circles around the empty roadway. Papa walked along, keeping up a good pace and secretly savoring his children's joy.

The Browns were glad to see them. Mary Alice quickly put on some milk to warm for hot chocolate, which would be ready after they cut the tree. Arch threw on his big mackinaw overcoat and hat, grabbed his sled and saw, and headed down the trail into the woods with Papa, the children following at their heels.

"O, Christmas tree, O, Christmas tree, which one will we be cutting," sang Elizabeth. "A balsam or a tall white pine, a blue spruce or another kind?"

"Mother prefers a balsam," said Francis.

"Yes," said Papa, "we'll look for a balsam first." And they found one not far along the path.

Harry said, "Smell the needles. That's how Mother says you tell. What are they s'posed to smell like?"

"Balsam!" said Thomas, laughing out loud at his cleverness.

"Oh," said Harry, not yet old enough to understand that they were making fun of him.

"Is it full enough?" asked Archie.

"I think it will be all right," said Thomas. "It has one little empty spot, but we'll put that up to the corner." They all agreed and Papa and Francis used Archie's saw to cut it down.

When they got back to the house, they drank their cocoa with great haste and headed out into the cold again. Archie walked with Papa while the boys pulled the tree on the sled. Harry was dragging behind, so Papa picked him up and put him on the sled. He rode in the sweet smelling, soft balsam boughs all the way to the wharf.

"I know the smell now, Thomas," he announced on arrival. "I'll tell Mother that I c'n find a balsam now if she needs one."

Francis and Thomas retrieved all of the packages from the store and found that Mother's Sears and Roebuck order had arrived at the post office, as well. On top of that, a great package had arrived, as it did each year, from the Maine Seacoast Missionary Society. The children knew that this package held a gift for everyone on Jib. With all of this freight, Papa knew they could never get everything and themselves back in one trip. He was anxious to get the voyage underway because of the shortness of the daylight.

"Francis, you and Thomas will have to wait here with the tree while I take the packages and your sister and brother back. I'll be back for you as soon as I can."

"Yes, Pa," replied Francis. "We'll wait at the store."

They loaded with great speed and Papa drove the Christmas-laden boat, riding a bit low in the water, out across the bay.

Mother had been watching anxiously and came out on the porch to greet them, as it was getting even colder and would be dark in less than two hours. She hustled Harry inside and let Papa and Elizabeth pile the packages next to the boat shed. Papa headed back for the mainland in a hurry.

Francis and Thomas had walked down from the store and were waiting for Papa, as they knew just how long it would take. They loaded the tree and themselves into the boat, with a few small purchases, and back they went to Jib, bouncing on the waves as fast as the boat could go. They arrived just at dusk and hauled the boat up the skids, securing it in the boathouse. They lashed the tree to the boathouse wall where it would remain until they were ready to decorate it.

*   *   *   *

And that day came after what seemed to the children an eternity of waiting. The family decorated the tree with ornaments saved from over the years. Elizabeth could look at it and see a star she had made with one of the traveling schoolteachers when she was five or six. Thomas and Francis saw their paper chain from two years earlier. This year, Elizabeth helped Harry string the popcorn for decoration, and they used the extra balsam, cut from the bottom of the tree, to form a wreath for the door. They hung it on the inside of the house because it surely would have blown away.

Finally, Christmas Eve came. The children were as excited as could be. Mother, Papa, Nana, and the children went into the living room to sit near the tree. Some packages were already in place, nestled under the branches, awaiting the eager fingers that would unwrap them early the next morning. The children looked at each, trying to guess the contents. Papa took Harry on his lap and asked Francis to bring the Bible to him. He opened to the Gospel according to Saint Luke and began to read.

> And it came to pass in those days, that there went out a decree from Caesar Augustus that all the world should be taxed. … And Joseph also went up from Galilee, out of the city of Nazareth, into Judea, unto the city of David which is called Bethlehem, because he was of the house and lineage of David, to be taxed with Mary his espoused wife, being great with child.

Elizabeth looked at her mother, who was beginning to look "great with child." She thought about the new baby. *Were Joseph and Mary worried about having a baby? Mary was so young, maybe not too much older than she was. She knew they didn't have a doctor. They just had to trust in God and believe that He would take care of them.*

I guess if they could trust in God, and Mother and Papa can trust in God, then I can, too. I think I will start right now and trust that this will work out all right. I only hope God plans to give me a sister.

The children went off to sleep on Christmas Eve while "visions of sugarplums danced in their heads." Mother and Papa were content to sleep for a while, with Papa always ready to check on the light.

Christmas morning came early. At about five o'clock Harry came into Elizabeth's room. "Lizzie," he whispered, "can we go down now?"

"Shhhh," said Elizabeth, "Don't wake Nana up. I think it is too early."

"No, it's not," said Thomas, who had crept in after Harry. "It's five-fifteen and we're allowed to go down at five-thirty. So that's only a few minutes. Get your bathrobes and slippers; I'll get Francis." As soon as Francis arrived, he declared the time to be close enough and led the others to the living room, where he lit the lamp.

The sight of the lush tree with its multicolored decorations flickering in the pre-dawn light was a wonder. The lamplight reflected off of the metal icicles and gilded balls. The shiny red cranberries were deep and bright. The children exhaled a soft "aahhhh," followed by squeals and screams of delight.

Mother and Papa arrived in the living room at the moment Harry saw his surprise in front of the Christmas tree. A circle of wooden track held a little engine, eight freight cars, and three passenger cars. It looked just like the train Nana came on from Boston. It had been carved from wood and painted black and green, with the lettering "Boston and Maine" on the sides.

Harry dropped down on his stomach with his elbows on the rug, supporting his head in his hands and staring at the beautiful engine. "B, O, S, T, O, N … M, A, I, N, E. Boston and Maine, Papa, just like the real ones." He reached out and touched the top of the engine, pulling it gently along the track. "Chuga, chuga, chuga, chuga, whoo a whoo, whoo a whoo. All aboard for Boston, all aboooaarrd." Harry began to make up the story of his Christmas journey, which would last all the day long and end only when Papa carried him, still clutching his engine, up the stairs to bed.

Thomas appointed himself the present-passer and stationed himself next to the tree. "Here's something for Francis," he said, holding up a large package tied with red ribbon.

"Probably long underwear." Elizabeth looked at Nana and rolled her eyes.

"No, it's not," said Harry. "I know …"

"Shhhh, Harry!" said Elizabeth. "Don't tell!"

Francis pulled off the ribbon and tore at the wrapping. He was amazed as the beautiful quilt unfolded itself and reached to the floor.

"I thought you were making quilts for the baby," said Francis with wide eyes.

"We were," answered Nana, "And we were making one for you, too."

"Yeah," said Harry, "and I cut the pinwheels. They're really triangles put together. Did ya know that, Francis? Huh? Did ya? I'll show you how it works …"

"Here's something for you to open, Mother," said Francis as he placed a small parcel in her lap. Mother carefully unwrapped the gift.

It was a carved rattle with a delicate latticework encasing several small wooden balls. When she shook the rattle, it made pleasant soft noises.

"Did you carve this, Francis?"

"Yup, Arch has been teaching me some of the fancier stuff he learned when he was out at sea. Some of the men did this kind of carving with whalebone, but I only had wood. Ya carve the little balls right inside of the cage."

"Let me look at that, son," said Papa, admiring the fine workmanship.

"So that's what you were carving, said Thomas. "Let me see."

Finally, it was Elizabeth's turn. Thomas put a box in front of her on the floor. It was wrapped in brown paper with colored decorations and cutouts from catalogs stuck to the paper.

"I wrapped it, Lizzie. Isn't it beautiful? Isn't it?" asked Harry.

Elizabeth didn't say anything. As she lifted the tissue paper, she couldn't believe her eyes. The red wool of the coat was the color of the cranberries strung on the tree. The black buttons were carved like rosebuds. She lifted the gift out of the box and held it up. The darts pulled in the waist, which then flared out. The black fur collar matched the fur on the padded muff, and the red hat was trimmed with fur, too. Speechless, she looked from her father to her mother and then to Nana, who was quietly enjoying Elizabeth's pleasure.

"You made this, didn't you?"

"Well, I had a lot of help. Francis shot the foxes and Mary Alice dyed the pelts. Your Papa carved the buttons and Thomas painted them. Your mother helped me cut and made the lining. So, you see, it was a family project. We didn't want you to go off to high school without a proper coat."

Elizabeth fell into her grandmother's arms and hugged her tiny body. "Mercy me, child, don't break me in two; I am looking forward to my dinner."

"Hey, Lizzie, I got you a present, too," said Harry. "Here."

Elizabeth unwrapped the tissue paper roll and found a new issue of a magazine about travel to far-off places.

"Just what I wanted, Harry. It's perfect."

*   *   *   *

All enjoyed a Christmas dinner of goose with all the trimmings, and the day ended with a delightfully exhausted bunch of Barton children climbing or being carried off to bed.

In the days that followed, Mother prepared for her trip to the mainland to await the birth of the newest member of the family. Packing was completed and instructions were given to Francis, Elizabeth and Thomas. Mother made lists of things and where to find them and made sure that Elizabeth understood the important recipes. Elizabeth fought back tears each day as they made more preparations.

And so, on the very first good day after Christmas, Papa took Mother and Nana to the mainland, where Mother was settled in the Browns' guestroom and Nana climbed on the train for Boston.

Now Elizabeth was in charge at the Lightkeeper's House on Jib Island all by herself. Jib seemed desolate to Elizabeth as she was the only girl in the house.

Can I do this? Can I keep this house the way Mother does? Can I keep the boys and Papa and Harry fed and warm? Can I? Can I? I just don't know.

*   *   *   *

The days passed quickly after the holidays. Elizabeth fell, exhausted, into her bed each night after taking care of all of the kitchen chores and trying to keep up with her schoolwork as well.

"Papa, I do not know how Mother does all this work every day. No wonder she was so tired."

"Taking care of a family is a great deal of work, Lizzie. You are doing an excellent job! Can the boys help you any more than they are?"

"They are doing pretty well, Papa, as long as they remember to take their boots off and not muddy the floor. They don't seem to be complaining about my cooking."

"They had better not!" said Papa. "You are quite a cook for your age. I guess you had a fine teacher."

"I miss Mother so much, Papa."

"I know. We all do. But you probably more than the rest of us, as you carry the burden of her work. It won't be too much longer. Stay strong," said Papa.

CHAPTER TWELVE

Shipwreck

Elizabeth, Francis, and Thomas stood with mouths agape at the top of the hill overlooking Summer Beach. They could not believe their eyes. Thomas was the first to speak.

"Holy cow! How did that happen, Papa?"

"It looks like some careless giant threw it away after play, and it landed on the beach all broken," Papa said soberly.

The *Horton* had washed up on Jib during the night at the tail end of the storm. It rested slightly on its port side at the tip of the north end of the island under the great rocks, which had dealt the graceful sailor its final blow. Its mainmast was intact but all the rigging was in a wild tangle, and there were broken timbers tossed here and there and frozen in the ice.

Papa had gone out early and alone to look the island over after the tempest. He soon came into the kitchen with a determined stride and reached for the radio. Papa never came across the kitchen floor with wet boots.

"Hello, Ervin?" He said to the man at the Coast Guard station.

"Schooner *Horton* washed up on Jib last night." He listened to the Coast Guard officer.

"Ship is the Horton, H-O-R-T-O-N. Don't know where she's from," he answered.

"No, don't see a sign of anyone a'tall."

"Uh-huh, I will. You boys can't get to us yet, and looks like there's no hurry. I'll go out and look around s'more. Right. Right. I'll check in later." Papa hung up the phone and looked over at the children, who had listened intently.

They were still as snowmen. Their spoons stuck up straight in the porridge they had been eating when Papa came in. They hadn't taken another bite. Thomas broke the silence.

"A wreck, Papa? Can we go with you, please?"

"Please, Pa?" echoed Francis. They seemed not to breathe as they waited for their father's reply. But Thomas couldn't control himself for very long.

"Maybe we'll find treasure," he whispered, his eyes looking a bit wild.

"The contents of the ship belong to the ship's owners, Thomas, not to us," stated Papa firmly. "But you and Francis may go out with me, if you like."

Elizabeth's face at once lost its eagerness and her chin dropped. Just as quickly she raised her eyes to look at her father and spoke boldly.

"And me, too, Papa?"

"And me, too, Papa?" echoed Harry.

Father hesitated. "Well, I guess we could ask Mrs. Guptil to watch Harry for a while. Mother wouldn't approve, but … okay, Lizzie, you, too." He winked at her and she glowed back at him. Harry shot his lower lip out and stamped his foot.

"Shush, Harry. No one is going without a full stomach," said Papa as he spooned some porridge into his bowl from the pot that had been simmering on the stove and sat down at the table with the children, who were devouring their lukewarm oatmeal. They finished in seconds, taking huge gulps of the glue-like mush.

Then Thomas asked, "Was there no one on the ship, Pa?"

"Didn't see a soul. Walked around it. Seems positively wedged in the ice and rocks and not breaking up anymore. There's a hole in the bow and I crawled in and called, but heard no voices."

"What was she carrying?" asked Francis.

"Not sure yet. Most've it's been washed out."

"Is it spooky, Pa?" Thomas's eyes were wide and bright. Papa gave Elizabeth a quick wink that Thomas couldn't see and then turned to him.

"Well, Thomas, there were some noises I just couldn't account for when I was lookin' into that hole in her side. I guess we'll have to look sharp."

Thomas spoke quietly. "I'd love to see a ghost." He sat trancelike looking out the kitchen window.

Papa got up from the table and went to one of the high shelves in the pantry. He reached up and took down some small lanterns and gave them to Francis.

"You each might need a lantern, and Francis, you carry some extra candles and matches. We'll stay together as much as possible." Papa went out the kitchen door and in a few minutes came back with a rope. The children had their boots, coats, and hats on by the time he returned. The empty dishes sat silently on the kitchen table with the spoons still in them. Papa tied one end around his waist and then tied each of the children into the rope so they were all attached. He left plenty of line in between them so they could move around easily.

"Thomas, you be at the end, then Lizzie will be between you."

Harry dragged his coat over to Elizabeth. "Get me ready, too, Lizzie."

"You have to stay with Mrs. Guptil, son." Papa's voice was definite.

"Why can't I go?" He sniffled a little.

Elizabeth comforted him. "It's too long a walk for you in this wind, Harry. And it isn't going to be a lot of fun. We'll probably have to carry heavy stuff back with us. You'll do better playing with Freddy and Sam. Don't fuss now; Papa is ready to go." Harry pouted quietly. She had finished buttoning up his coat and pulling on his warm stocking cap and mittens. She stuffed her own mittens in her pockets. Papa made the call to Mrs. Guptil and then waited by the door.

Thomas was the first one ready. He was wiggling all over like a puppy hoping to play ball. He pelted Papa with questions.

"What if we find someone, Pa? Can the Coast Guard get here before dark? Will the ship break up or just stay on the island? Can we use it for firewood? Does …"

"Thomas, Thomas, no more of this. We'll see when we get there." As soon as Papa opened the back door, Thomas bolted out, heading straight for the path to the north end of Jib. He forgot he was attached and was stopped sharply as he got to the end of his rope.

"Hold on there, boy!" Papa yelled. "You are to go behind Elizabeth and be the rear guard!" Thomas shot a hard glance at Elizabeth, who ignored it.

They all trudged over to the Assistant Keeper's house and deposited an unhappy Harry with Mrs. Guptil. Then they set out. Papa was in the front, followed by Francis, Elizabeth, and then Thomas, clipping her heels.

The wind was strong with biting gusts and they were heading into its full force. Francis's long arms were hanging from his short coat sleeves and he pulled up his mittens and plunged his hands deeply into his pockets to protect his forearms. Elizabeth pulled her hat down over her forehead and tied it securely. Her fingers were tingling by the time she got her mittens on. Even Nana's warmest double-knits weren't enough in this weather. She couldn't put her hands in her pockets because she needed all the arm motion she could muster to keep up with Francis's long strides. Thomas seemed oblivious to the wind and cold and, even with his shorter legs, he kept up his pace just inches behind Elizabeth. Going down the little hill by the pond, Elizabeth slipped and then regained her balance. Thomas couldn't keep from ramming into her, as he was so close behind.

She whirled around. "Thomas, give me some room. If I fall, you'll go right down with me." Thomas's brows closed down over his eyes in disgust.

They trudged through the snow and ice behind Papa, across the wide, high hill, and down by the cliff of the northwest inlet, out to the beach. From the sky they most likely looked like a procession of penguin chicks waddling after their mother. As they approached the north end of the island, Elizabeth saw the defeated ship *Horton* perched on the icy rocks like a toy model on display.

Elizabeth felt a heavy weight in her stomach and gasped as she watched the vicious waves beating on the stern. The slender black body looked like a dead person, powerless and at the mercy of the surrounding forces. It was wedged tightly in the ice and didn't budge, but some of the larger waves hit the frozen cliff and made sounds like thunder that echoed through the ship and screamed out a small hole in the stern. With every strike of a large wave, a piece of the ship's cargo could be seen bouncing in the white foam. They all stared.

"Oh, how awful," Francis murmured, his eyes solemn. "Papa, are you sure there are no survivors?"

"Saw no signs of any this morning. But we'll have another look."

"How could anyone have survived?" Elizabeth whispered to herself.

Papa picked his way over the ice-covered rocks to the gashed opening as they followed. Elizabeth's hand stung from grabbing the frozen roughness of the periwinkles that were sharp enough to push through her mittens. *What could it be like to be dashed on the rocks*, she asked herself. Her mittens seemed to weigh a pound each with the balls of frozen snow stuck to them. She pulled the icy residue off.

Papa reached the hole and turned to them. "You may not come in, children. Just keep watch for me. I am going to tie this rope around me and you will hold tight to it. I have my life jacket on as well, but you can pull me in if I get washed out."

"Pa, what if you find any dead people?" asked Thomas. Elizabeth shivered.

"Pray we don't," he said as he slid into the hole and was gone. The children watched the sea, the ship, and the rope without saying a word.

As Thomas was the last in line, and the others were focused on the hole in the ship, they did not see him untie the rope around his waist. He jumped to the beach and grabbed the rope near the hole. In a split second he was inside the ship.

"Thomas!" Elizabeth shrieked.

"Tom, you better get back here," Francis yelled. "You will be in such trouble."

It was no use. Francis and Elizabeth looked at each other in terror and they knew Papa would be more than furious with Thomas.

"We can't do anything but wait," said Elizabeth, "Papa will take care of him."

The two moved together to help each other hold the rope and

watch for their father to emerge.

"I can't believe he disobeyed Papa," Elizabeth finally said. "How could he do that, after all we have been taught?"

"He's always been impulsive, Lizzie! Maybe this will teach him something."

*   *   *   *

Inside the ship, Thomas moved slowly along the rope. He did not see his father, who was far ahead of him. He entered and looked around the room nearest him. It had been a large bunkroom once, but now the blankets were frozen with seawater and thrown in heaps on and off the bunks, which looked like closet shelves stacked with piles of messy clothing. A pair of blue sailor's pants hung from the post in the center of the room and a yellow oilskin jacket floated in a chunk of ice, which had settled where the deck met the hull. It was harder to walk here because the handholds in the hull sheathing were only on the side, and the deck was at a slight angle. As the ship shifted a bit underneath him, Thomas realized he had made a mistake.

He had to find Papa. He left the cabin and entered the passageway, then headed up another ladder. He could hardly see, as in his haste he had not brought his lantern. A bit of light was coming through the hole in the stern and as he climbed higher he entered a sunlit passage.

"Thomas! What are you doing in here? I told you to wait outside with the others."

Thomas turned to face his father. "I'm sorry, Papa. I really lost good sense and came in after you."

"We can't deal with your behavior now. Stay with me and we will get out of here as soon as we can. And mind me to the letter, young man."

"Yes, sir," said Thomas.

"I must check the captain's cabin and see if I can find the log. Then we will go back out. You watch where I step and put your feet in the same spots," said Papa.

They walked slowly along the passageway to the stern and found the captain's quarters. It was not as wet in this cabin. The blankets on the bed appeared to be dry. Papa approached the desk and looked for the log. He found it in the desk drawer; it was dry too.

"I found it. Good, now we can go."

Just as they turned to go, Thomas tripped on a chair, which had overturned on the deck of the cabin. As he fell, his head struck the corner of the captain's desk and he jerked away, landing on the captain's berth. Papa reached down and tried to grab the boy's coat, but then lost his grip and Thomas fell onto the pile of bedclothes. He sank into the jumble of sheets on the large berth that slanted toward the side of the ship. Papa leaned down with his ear to Thomas's nose and mouth and reached one of his square hands into Thomas's coat.

"Thomas, can you hear me? "

The boy seemed very small in his silence. His lips were the purple color they displayed during those rare July swimming sessions. His hair was matted to his head like a close-fitting cap and his skin was as gray-white as the feathers of a gull.

Papa rubbed the boy's hands and face and tried to wake him. At first Thomas didn't respond. Then Papa heard a weak moan coming from the boy. His eyes blinked slightly and then closed.

"Ooohhh! My head." Thomas squeezed his eyes shut. His hand pushed Papa's away. "Ooohhh, don't touch!" Papa pulled his hand away.

"Ooohhh, please, Papa, leave my head alone."

"I'm not touching your head, Thomas."

"My head hurts, Papa. And someone's hitting my back."

"You're just confused, Thomas. You had quite a bad fall."

"Stop hitting my head," Thomas screamed, his eyes still shut tight. "Leave me alone."

Just then Papa noticed that the blankets underneath Thomas were moving, rising up from the bed as if a ghost were beginning to materialize. He stared at the spot as the sheet moved. It looked as if there was an arm underneath.

"Hold on, Thomas!" said Papa as he reached behind the boy to the pile of blankets and pulled them away. A round shape appeared to be underneath the sheet. Papa froze.

"Please, stop poking me!" yelled Thomas. He opened his eyes and looked up at Papa. He could see that Papa was not touching him.

"Ouch," he said. Then his eyes opened wider and wider.

"Pa, there is something moving underneath me." Thomas fainted.

Papa reached down and picked Thomas up, cradling the limp head close to his thick coat. Papa's eyes were riveted to the bed as the blankets and sheets continued to move and, within seconds, from out of the tangled mass appeared some thin fingers, followed by a hand, and then a small white arm. As soon as the arm had created an opening between the covers, Papa found himself face to face with a small girl who had a mass of bright red hair and so many freckles that she looked like a bowl of cream swarmed over with flies.

"Please," she said weakly, "I'm very cold."

CHAPTER THIRTEEN

Stranger

The redheaded girl lay quiet and white-faced on Elizabeth's bed, under Nana's quilt. The great light lit the room with slow, intermittent brightness. It was as if it were watching over the child, beating as her heart continued to beat and breathing as she continued to breathe.

Elizabeth sat on the bed, too, staring at the girl. She didn't consciously think about the comfort of her light, but she felt it. Whatever or whoever protected this young girl somehow was not able to save the rest of the crew.

Elizabeth wondered about the sailors. She pictured them floating lifeless in the murky ocean bottom. Then she imagined them swimming, swimming south toward Barbados. There they were, the whole crew and the captain, swimming in the blue-green waters of the Caribbean. They were safe now and could even breathe underwater. *That must be where heaven is for sailors,* she thought, *the lovely, sandy bottom of the Caribbean, with beautiful fish to watch and play with.*

Her mind came back to the little stranger. Elizabeth didn't even know the girl's name, and she was afraid that the girl might join the sailors. She was afraid of all the possibilities: *Will she wake up? What if she doesn't? What if she does and she's sick for a long time? Will I ever know who she is?*

She tucked extra blankets around the child's body and spooned goose broth into her mouth. Papa had allowed her to call Mother and ask for specific instructions.

"Hello, hello, Mother?"

"Yes, Lizzie. Is everything all right?"

"Yes, Mother, we're fine, but there was a shipwreck and the ship landed on Jib, Mother, and we went on it and we found a little girl. She was the only one on it and she's alive. She's asleep and I'm trying to take care of her. What should I do, Mother? I want her to wake up. I'm afraid she might die."

Mother understood that Elizabeth had every reason to be afraid.

"Lizzie, the most important thing is to get her body warm, but it has to be done slowly. Rub her hands and feet every fifteen minutes or so, and then work up her arms and her legs. Heat the bricks and keep them around her at the edge of the bed, not too close for now. Fill up the hot water bottle and put it under her pillow. As the bricks cool, get warm ones. Open a jar of broth, warm it, only warm, not hot, and spoon some into her every hour."

Mother went on with her instructions. Before the end of their conversation, she added one final, but important, thought.

"Lizzie, dear, remember, if the little girl doesn't wake up, it's not your fault. It is really in God's hands now. He doesn't expect you to do anything other than what you know to do and neither does anyone else. God alone knows if that child will live on earth or in heaven, and it's His choice, not ours, so don't you fret about what you're doing. You're a good and capable girl, Lizzie, but the outcome isn't your responsibility."

Mother paused. "I'm sorry I'm not there to help you with this, Lizzie. I love you very much."

"I love you, too, Mother."

"Let me talk to your Papa, then, dear."

"Sure, Mother. Bye-bye."

Papa took the phone and spoke briefly with Mother. Mostly he said, "Yes," and "I will, Hildy, try not to worry," and "I know, I know." At the end he whispered, but Lizzie heard him say, "I love you, too, Hildy."

Papa hung up the phone and turned to the children. "We need to stay up all night with the little girl. Francis, you will take the shift right after supper to let Lizzie get some sleep. I will wake you and take over, and then Lizzie will be ready to stay with her in the morning. Francis, you will clean up after dinner with Harry's help so Lizzie can go right to bed." Papa had called the doctor, but he was unable to get there until the seas were more manageable.

Thomas was sporting a small lump on the top of his head, but seemed to be undamaged otherwise. Papa had been stern with Thomas for disobeying him, but he couldn't be angry, because if Thomas had obeyed, they wouldn't have found the girl.

The children quietly ate the supper Lizzie had cooked. They were all tired from their excitement and afraid for the little girl.

"Pa, is the Coast Guard trying to find out who she is?" asked Francis. "Does it take a long time to trace a ship?"

"They are working on it, Francis. Maybe we'll hear tomorrow. My guess is that she was related to someone on the ship. We found some of her clothes in the captain's cabin, so my guess is she was connected to the captain, somehow," answered Papa.

"Do you think she sailed to Barbados a lot?" quizzed Lizzie.

"She had mostly summer clothes with her on the boat. I'd guess she's been there more than once."

Elizabeth's mind slipped into daydreams of a little girl sailing on a splendid ship in the gentle, tropical seas, reclining on the warm deck, and snacking on lush fruit. *That life's all over for her now, even if she does wake up,* Elizabeth thought. *What will she do?*

After supper, she went up to sleep in the spare room. Francis watched over the patient and Thomas and Harry cleaned up the dishes.

*   *   *   *

"Wake up, Lizzie," Papa said quietly as he shook her arm. It was sunrise and he was ready to go out to the light. "Our little visitor is still asleep, but she's alive. Go get dressed now and get some more broth for her. Check the bricks and hot water bottle; I changed them several hours ago."

"She's alive, Papa. That's a good sign, isn't it?

"It is a good sign, Lizzie. But she's not out of the woods yet. Now up you get." He lifted her out of the bed and swung her around, placing her gently on the covers but outside their warmth. He kissed the top of her head and went quickly down the stairs and out the door. Elizabeth snatched her clothes from the chair and dressed, hopped down to the kitchen and warmed up some broth.

She took broth to the sleeping child and spooned it gently into her mouth. She wasn't sure how much was swallowed and how much dribbled on the towel she had tucked under the girl's chin. Then she sat back in the chair, sipping some tea and eating her own porridge, which Papa had left on the stove. She watched the little freckled face as she ate and became lost in her thoughts.

She thought about little Jenny, whom they couldn't make well. She thought about her mother on the mainland, waiting in bed for the birth of the new child. She wanted her mother here with her, helping to care for this sick child. *I just don't know enough,* she thought. *What if I do the wrong thing? What if the doctor doesn't get here?*

Elizabeth reached under the covers and massaged the little girl's feet and legs, and then went on to her hands and arms. She took the tray and dishes down to the kitchen.

The kitchen was empty. Harry was over at the Guptils' and Thomas and Francis were out helping Papa and Mr. Guptil salvage things from the ship. The day was clearing, but the sky was the steel blue of a frozen pond. She looked out of the kitchen window at the lighthouse. It stood white and unmoving; it was perfect and all-powerful. For the first time in all her twelve years she really thought she hated living on this isolated island, where everything was controlled by the needs of that lighthouse. *Stupid thought,* she reprimanded herself. *Think of the people who would die without that light. How selfish can I be?* Although she knew that the light had failed to save the *Horton.*

She climbed the stairs to her room under the weight of the bricks and of her thoughts. She wrapped the bricks in a small blanket and tucked them in the bed under the little girl's white, icy feet. She thought she felt one of the legs move over toward the warm brick, and looked up quickly to see if there was any change in her face. It was unchanged.

I wonder who she is, and where she's from. Papa says the boat was from Nova Scotia, but it had been to Barbados. Is she from Nova Scotia or

Barbados? I can't wait 'til she wakes up so I can talk to her. She looks almost my age. Well, maybe not. She might only be ten, but I don't care. I've never had a girl around who was even close to twelve. I hope she can stay forever and be my sister. Oh, please, please wake up so we can talk!

But Elizabeth's wishing was useless; the girl simply slept.

Elizabeth remembered helping Mother and Nana take care of Francis once when he had gotten too cold on a duck-hunting trip. She remembered that he had slept a long time. She tried to remember all the things they had done for him, and then she knew she was taking good care of her patient. She had dressed her in the warmest flannel night-gown. She had put several blankets on her and topped them off with Nana's quilt. Then she remembered that Nana sat and rocked and sang softly to Francis, hymns mostly. So she sang very softly to this very small face with the very prominent, rust-colored freckles.

> *This is my Father's world,*
> *I rest me in the thought*
> *Of rocks and trees, of skies and seas,*
> *His hands the wonders wrought.*

*   *   *   *

Nana had written to Lizzie at the New Year to tell her about the holiday decorations in Boston that were still up through early January and about the concert of beautiful music she had gone to at Symphony Hall. She had heard a piece by a Russian composer, Igor Stravinsky. Elizabeth read quietly from this letter to the little girl while she slept.

"The store windows are filled with mannequins dressed in the latest fashions and wrapped in ropes of holly. One window has children playing around a Christmas tree decorated with many shiny glass balls and cupids and dolls dressed in velvet and lace. They have new toys around them, including a building set made of pieces of metal of various shapes with holes in each piece. The pieces can be connected with nuts and bolts, and the children are constructing all kinds of items with them. One boy made a car and another made a boat."

Nana told her that the toy was called an erector set and was invented by a man named Mr. Gilbert. Nana thought she might save up to get an erector set for the Bartons next Christmas.

"The people in my apartment have decorated as well and, Elizabeth, you won't believe this, but old Mr. Codfish even said, 'Happy New Year!'"

Elizabeth smiled when she read about Mr. Codfish. She also had a letter from Mother that arrived the day before the storm on the supply boat.

"My dear Elizabeth," she wrote, "I am comfortably settled here with our dear friends, and they are so kind to me. The doctor has visited and says that I may get up once or twice a day for a short time, and I do look forward to those moments. I helped Mary Alice make some biscuits today. It was good to feel useful. I thought about your making all the biscuits for Papa and the boys. What comfort it gives me to know that you can do so many things. I will not completely rest until I am back on Jib with my darling children. Much love to you all, your Mother."

I will not rest until you are back with us, Mother, Elizabeth thought. *I'll do my best, but I really need you, Mother. I'm twelve and I know you think I can do so much, and I am trying, really, but you're the mother, not me, and I'm tired now. I'm really tired.*

The day was long. The doctor had called to say that he would not be able to get to Jib at all and that they were doing all the right things to help the little girl. Francis came back by mid-afternoon, and Mrs. Guptil came over after dinner to help out. She brought some fresh biscuits and fish chowder. Elizabeth put the food together and fed the boys supper, cleaned up, and then, by about ten, she went back to the spare room and slept soundly.

She woke again at four in the morning. The hours of sleep had been short as Elizabeth sat dozing by the little girl. Was she still dozing when she saw the small, twinkling light through the window. What made her wake up and notice it? It was not the bright strands of light from the big light, but simply a candle flame or lamplight moving closer from the open sea. She watched it dance toward her. It could be a star falling slowly toward her, sliding across the frozen sky like a runaway sled.

"Now, really, Elizabeth," she scolded herself. It could be a light from the mast of a ship coming too close to Jib. But the way it danced and skipped, it looked for all the world like a lantern being thrown and tossed by the wind, but not being blown out. She watched it, trying to discover the light's origin. *Where is it coming from? Where is it going? It seems to be moving slowly, but heading straight for my window, and that is not possible. This is the second floor!*

Possible or not, the light kept coming, and it now seemed so strange that Elizabeth felt a chill catch her in the small of her back and creep up toward her neck. She stood frozen, looking at the window, as the form of a tall man in the uniform of a ship's captain approached her with steady steps. She knew that this could not be happening, as his steps were taken on the empty space outside her window. Elizabeth was terrified, but then she saw the kind smile on his face. It calmed her and made her feel safe. Now she was simply wide-eyed in disbelief. His jacket and pants were a deep blue and the brass buttons shone as Papa's did before an inspection. His short beard was snow white and trimmed neatly, and his mustache was broad and razor straight. A clean, white cap rested firmly on his suntanned forehead and, as he lifted the lantern higher, Elizabeth could see the wrinkles on his dark face. His eyes were deep-set and very dark brown, so very dark brown that they seemed black.

She watched him and wondered if he would speak; she could not move to gesture or say a word. He looked at her with his kindly smile and then looked toward the bed where the unconscious girl lay. He watched the quiet face, encircled with red curls, for what seemed like endless moments, and then his free hand reached up to his mouth and he blew a kiss toward the little girl. He looked at Elizabeth, smiled at her kindly, and turned around. In a few seconds he was lost to her in the wind that whipped by. She looked at the girl briefly then stared out at the black sky.

Elizabeth pinched herself to see if she was awake. *Did she really see this distinguished visitor come to her window and look in on them, and smile at them? What would Papa say when she told him what had happened? Should she tell him at all? She certainly wouldn't tell Francis or Thomas, as they would laugh and hoot and tease her forever. She wished Nana were here. She knew she could trust Nana to listen to her story.* For right now, Elizabeth decided to tell no one. She slept sitting in the chair with her head and arms resting on the foot of the bed.

Soon it was dawn and Papa came to the room to check on the little girl. She still slept quietly; her breathing was steady, but so quiet that it was hard to see any movement in her body. Papa had brought warm bricks and a fresh hot water bottle.

"I think it's time for some more broth, Elizabeth, and in a little while, let's try some warm sweet tea."

Elizabeth went slowly down to the kitchen, her mind full of the past night's happenings. She warmed some broth for the little girl and toasted a biscuit for herself.

Did the captain really walk through the air and look in my window? Who was he? Why did he blow a kiss to the little girl? The questions whirled around in her head. She brought the food back upstairs on a tray, which she set on the bureau.

Papa was sitting in the chair, holding the little girl's hand and talking to her in a low voice. "Who might you be, little lass? And where are you from? It should be time for you to wake, shouldn't it? Don't be afraid. We'll care for you. Don't be afraid to wake up."

Elizabeth watched her father and put her arms around his neck from behind. "Do you think she will wake up, Papa? Do you?"

"When I rubbed her feet just now, they moved a little from my touch. They feel a bit warmer. I'm hopeful, with reservations, but hopeful. I must go back now," he said. He held Elizabeth for a long hug and then left the room and took the stairs down two by two.

Elizabeth spooned the broth into the small bluish lips and wiped the spills from the tiny chin with a towel. The little girl's face grimaced a bit. "Oh, my," said Elizabeth, "are you waking?" But the little face resumed its composure and became perfectly still.

It was not quite dawn, but Elizabeth was watching for another sign of awakening. This time when she saw the light approach the window, she knew she was awake. She watched intently as the captain came close to the windowpane and watched the little girl. He smiled kindly at Elizabeth and held the lantern up high so as to see clearly into the room. This time he nodded to Elizabeth and put his finger to his lips as if asking for silence, and then turned and disappeared.

Elizabeth did not move. She looked out the window and watched for another sign of him. *I know I was awake; I know I was. I was awake.*

CHAPTER FOURTEEN

The Awakening

I t was before dawn when the redheaded girl began to stir in Elizabeth's bed. She did not move her head, just her eyes. She felt warm and the quilt over her smelled of lavender.

Where am I? I'm not on the Horton—the bed is dry and smells nice. Where could I be? How did I get here? I don't remember. Where is Grandfather?

The light was flashing slowly but steadily in the windows across from the bed, but the room was quiet. When the little girl felt a leg move beside her, she realized there was someone else in the bed. She was afraid. She squeezed her eyes tight, then dozed off and on for what seemed like hours, but was in reality only minutes. When she awoke again, the room was brighter. The legs moved again and a person sat up, tucked the quilt around the little girl, then hopped out of bed and left the room.

The freckled-face girl opened her eyes again and moved her head so she could see around the room. It was an ordinary room with white walls, a dresser, a coat rack, a wash stand, and this bed. It had two windows and the light outside was still flashing on and off.

I don't like it here. Why is the light flashing? Grandfather will wake up soon. He will come and find me and take me back to the Horton.

She turned on her side, away from the door, wriggled herself down under the quilt, and fell back to sleep.

*   *   *   *

When Elizabeth came back to her bed after pumping water into the big kettle and putting it on the stove to prepare for breakfast, she saw that the little girl was still asleep. Elizabeth's feet were cold from the icy floor, but the warm bed soon relaxed her and she slept again. When she woke, the house was still quiet, so Elizabeth reached for her magazine from the floor and began to read. She watched the little girl's quiet face, read a little, and then dozed off once more.

Elizabeth was in a light slumber when when the bundle under the blankets turned over toward her. Elizabeth opened her eyes and thought for an instant that she saw two little eyes open and close again under a pile of red curls. She watched for a minute to see if they would open again. They did not, but she did see movement underneath the eyelids and she knew the sign. Harry always tried to pretend he was napping, but when his eyes moved behind the lids, he couldn't fool Elizabeth.

Her heart started to pound as she reached her hand over to the freckled forehead and felt its warmth. She brushed the red curls away from the small face and spoke softly, trying to sound like Mother.

"Hello, little girl. Good morning to you! How are you feeling?"

*   *   *   *

The little girl squeezed her eyes closed, shutting out wherever this new place was. She tightened all her face muscles, making a protective mask against the intrusion of the voice. It seemed like a strange voice. She had not heard the voices of young girls very often. Boys voices were quite different.

Where is this place? Why am I here? I don't remember Grandfather leaving me back on the mainland. Am I with those people in Halifax, the ones he'd threatened to board me with? How was I left with them without my knowing it? Where is Grandfather? Am I simply dreaming and will I wake up soon. She tightened her eyes and tried to go back to sleep.

*   *   *   *

Elizabeth watched the girl's eyes. She sat up, waiting. They will be bright and blue, she thought, to go with her beautiful red hair. The little girl was restless and Elizabeth knew she was awake and would soon have to open her eyes. All of a sudden, the girl blinked. The long, dark lashes fluttered for a moment and then the lids lifted until Elizabeth was looking straight into the darkest brown eyes she had ever seen. They were so dark that they were almost black. She jumped back as the fiery eyes accosted her. The dark eyebrows were knit into the angriest frown possible for such an angelic face. From within that angel, a human thunderstorm of a voice emerged in loud wails.

"I want my grandfather! Bring him here now! I want my grandfather!" Then she glared at Elizabeth and growled, "You know better than to disobey me. Go and get him this instant!" She began to scream a most blood-curdling scream, throwing herself around in the bedclothes.

Elizabeth was speechless. She had not expected such behavior from the sweet form she had nursed and guarded. *What could be the matter with this child? Even Harry never screamed like this.*

Elizabeth ran out of the room and down the stairs, looking for her father and the boys, but no one was in the house. She saw the shed door open and ran outside toward it with her nightgown flying and her bare feet not even feeling the icy ground.

"Papa, Paaapaa! Come quickly. Come now!" said Elizabeth as she ran.

"What is it, little one?" Papa said, as he came out of the shed.

His strong arms reached out for her and caught her around her slender waist, holding her as she wriggled and tried to talk in breathless gasps.

"She's a-awake. She's alive. She's screaming and wild. You must come."

"She's made it, has she? That's wonderful!" said Papa with a wide smile.

"You might not think so when you see her," said Elizabeth as she pulled her father along as fast as she could, into the house, up the stairs, down the hallway, and around the corner to her room.

The small, redheaded waif was not the least bit changed, even with the sight of this large man looking down at her.

"You get my grandfather immediately," she said. "If you don't bring him here, you will lose your job. We don't keep sailors on the *Horton* who do not obey orders."

Her arms were out of the covers now, creamy white with freckles bursting out all over. Her brown-black eyes glared at Papa. She was certain that she had never seen Will Barton before.

Who is this man? How dare he disobey me? He must know I am the captain's granddaughter. Grandfather will surely dock his wages.

She set her face in stony silence for a few seconds and then attacked. "You better tell me where I am and who you are. I have never seen either of you. I want my grandfather right now. You go and get him."

Papa realized that this child did not remember what had happened on the ship. She had no idea that her grandfather was dead and that all of the crew was gone as well. He had to tell her, but gently. He thought about it for a few moments.

I wonder why this child was on the ship. Why was she asking for her grandfather, not her mother or her father? I suppose a child might live on a ship with her grandfather if she had no other home. What if this poor child had no other family except her grandfather, and now he is gone, too?

Papa's face looked sad. They were all three quiet, Papa in his thinking, Elizabeth in her wondering, and the new child in her anger and also in her fear.

Finally, Papa began to speak. He spoke quietly and gently as he did when he was telling the children something very important. As he spoke, the little girl seemed to relax a bit. She even looked at him quickly and then returned to her stare.

"I don't work for your grandfather, child. I don't even know your grandfather. I tend this light station. Do you see the light tower out the window?"

She nodded.

"You know what lighthouses do, don't you?"

She nodded again.

"We try our best to keep the ships safe, especially in storms and high winds. Sometimes we can and sometimes we can't. Will you let me pick you up, child?"

The little girl nodded.

Papa reached down carefully and pulled back her covers. He slipped an arm under her knees and with the other cradled her shoulders. She was no heavier than a bit of wind and her muscles were weak. Her head fell against his shoulder and her red curls covered his cheek. He walked slowly over to the window, where she could see more of the island. Off at the edge of her view was the *Horton*, what was left of her, sitting on the icy rocks.

"That's where we found you, in the *Horton*, a few days ago. You were huddled under a pile of blankets in the captain's cabin. You said that you were cold and we were surprised that you were awake. We brought you here unconscious and put you to bed. Elizabeth has been nursing you and keeping you warm. Someone stayed with you all the time, hoping that you'd wake up."

"But, what did you do with G-Grandfather? Where is he?" she asked softly, not really wanting an answer.

"Child, I am sorry to say, you were the only one on the ship when we found her."

The little girl was still as a snowman and then her whole body went limp. All of a sudden she began her terrible screaming again. Father held her tightly and let her scream. When the screams subsided he placed her back in bed where she curled up and began to cry and whimper. He took Elizabeth out of the room.

"She's had a bad shock and we must get her to rest as much as possible. The doctor may be able to get here today, and then we can ask him what to do. We must not let her feel as if she has nowhere to go, so tell her that she may stay with us until we find her family. Talk to her, see if she will say her name, and get her to eat something. Come for me if she gets worse."

He held Elizabeth close to him for longer than he usually did. He held her, as long as when she was going away for a few days to the mainland.

"You've done a good job, Elizabeth. I'm very proud of you. You're going to be a fine woman, like your mother."

Elizabeth didn't actually see tears in Papa's eyes, but what she did see was a softness she had seen only a few times before in her life, as if he were about to cry, but didn't actually allow himself to.

She entered the room carefully and saw that the girl was completely under the covers. Her whimpering continued. Elizabeth sat on the bed and patted the huddled form with as much comfort as she could muster. Finally, the body lay still and Elizabeth uncovered her head so that she could breathe as she slept. Elizabeth thought it would be all right to go down to the kitchen and get some breakfast.

The kitchen was a sight to behold. No one had taken proper care of it since they began caring for their found child. Oh, there were some dishes washed and left to dry on the sink board, and the food had been put away. But the tabletop had been wiped in some peculiar way and still held a mass of crumbs. Elizabeth looked at the mess and sighed a deep sigh. She was already exhausted from watching over the little redheaded whirlwind, and now she had to clean up the kitchen.

She spied fresh biscuits on the stove and said to herself, *Good for Papa. He made fresh biscuits, at least! I may have to clean this place, but I'm going to eat first.*

She put two biscuits in the oven to warm and went to the cold pantry to get a great big glass of milk. She brought the biscuits, jam, and butter over to the table, pulled Mother's chair up to the end, and perched there over her feast. Elizabeth had almost forgotten to eat while she was caring for the sick child, and now she was ravenous.

She spread the butter thickly on one side of the biscuit and laid a big spoonful of blueberry jam on the other side. As the sweetened biscuit passed her lips to her tongue, she thought she had never tasted anything quite so delicious. She leaned back in her chair and savored a few minutes with just the warmth of the stove, the biscuit, and the clean winter sky outside the kitchen window. Then, suddenly, she bounced up and said, "Well, I may as well get started. No one else is going to clean this mess up!"

Elizabeth grumbled out loud a little as she began scrubbing the porridge pot. But as she got closer to finishing her work and once again the kitchen looked like it should, she began to hum a little and made up a little tune that she sang to the milk jug and the floor mop. Finally, she was finished and went upstairs to check on her patient.

The red curls spilled onto the pillow and the creamy cheeks had a bit of pink in them. Elizabeth had brought a tray with some biscuits and milk, plenty of butter, and blueberry jam. She watched for movement under the eyelids and, when she saw it, she said, "Hello little girl, how about some breakfast? Are you feeling hungry?"

"I am not hungry," came a voice from under the covers. "I won't eat until you find my grandfather. He's just lost. You'll see. He's just lost and he'll be here to get me as soon as he finds out where I am. You must call the Coast Guard and tell them I am here." She paused a little looking around. "W-where is here, anyway?"

Elizabeth smiled. She was thrilled that the girl had asked a question.

"Here is Jib Island. My family lives on Jib because my father takes care of the light. He works for the Lighthouse Service."

Knowing that her father had already called the Coast Guard, she went on. "But when we call the Coast Guard we need to tell them who we are looking for and who we have here who is looking, so what is your name?"

The little girl blinked, her eyes peeking out of the covers. "I'm … I'm Lucy," she said. "Lucy MacPherson. Tell them to find my grandfather, Captain Isaiah Stuart MacPherson of the ship *Horton*, sailing from Yarmouth, Nova Scotia."

Elizabeth placed the tray next to the bed. "Well Lucy MacPherson, I am going to tell my father, while you eat your breakfast. You're a big girl. I shouldn't have to feed you like a baby."

"What do you mean, feed me like a baby? Of course you don't have to feed me like a baby. I am nine years old and I feed myself quite nicely."

"Then get to it. I'll be back soon to take the tray away."

The two girls glared at each other. As Elizabeth left the room, Lucy grabbed the first biscuit and heaped on the butter and jam. Elizabeth ran out to the shed and reported to Papa what she had learned. He came into the house and called the Coast Guard.

"That's right, a little girl, nine years old. Says she was sailing with her grandfather, MacPherson out of Yarmouth on the *Horton*. Said before, no sign of any men on that ship. On their way? Good. Thought they'd be here by now. Oh. Okay, then."

"What's the matter, Papa? Why haven't they come yet?" asked Elizabeth.

"Two other ships in trouble in this area in that storm. They'll be doin' the best they can to get here later today."

Elizabeth followed Papa back up the stairs. Lucy was sitting up in bed looking out the window. As she turned to look at her visitors, she brushed the tears from her face.

"I want to go down to the boat. I want to look for Grandfather. He might be hurt and waiting for me to come."

Papa sat down on the bed beside the frightened little girl and put his arm around her.

"Look child, I have been through the ship. That's how I found you, but no one else is there, alive, injured or … or dead. You were all of life that we found on that ship."

"But I want to go, to see for myself. Grandfather always said it is best to see for yourself."

"You are right, little one, and as soon as the authorities come, we'll carry you down there to have a look. But don't get your hopes up, child. There's nobody there."

She began to cry again. "Can you look around the island, in case Grandfather is lost? Wi-will you try to find Grandfather's chest and the logs? He told me we must never lose the logs."

"Francis and Thomas and I have taken from the ship all that we could save, and we have put it in the barn for now to dry out. It will all be there when you are ready. We found the logs and they are safe."

Lucy looked up at Papa, her dark eyes flashing now with thanks. She slipped back under the covers and slept.

Elizabeth looked at her and at Papa. She, too, gave him a big hug. Returning to the kitchen with Elizabeth, Papa gave these instructions.

"The doctor will not be coming at all. Since she seems to be all right, there's no sense in his making the trip. It'll be a hard time for her for a while. Do what you can, Lizzie, but don't spoil her. It's clear she's had enough of spoilin'. Just let her rest and see that she drinks as much as possible—warm tea several times a day. Mrs. Guptil will have had her fill of old Harry by now, don't ya think? Go get him, girl, and try to keep him out of mischief! I've got to get back to the light now, but we'll be in for dinner."

Elizabeth put on her coat and hat and mittens. She walked along the path to the Guptils' house and found Harry playing in the kitchen with the boys. They had some toy trucks their fathers had made out of wood and were busy "working" on a big construction project all around Mrs. Guptil's feet.

"Vroooooom, vrooom," said Freddy.

"Outa my way, I gotta put this load down where you are," said Harry.

"Wait'll I'm done, mister," answered Freddy.

"Better hurry," said Harry, "I'm on a schedule, y'know."

"I'm on a schedule, too," said Elizabeth. "If you want any dinner, you'd better get your coat and boots on and come along."

"Don't bother, Elizabeth. Freddy'll be quieter playing with Harry than if he's only got to contend with his brother. Let him stay and have dinner with us. We'll walk him over just 'fore supper. He's been fine, Elizabeth, really," said Mrs. Guptil. Then she asked about the little girl, and Elizabeth told her all she knew.

"Poor little thing," Mrs. Guptil said. Elizabeth didn't exactly agree. As soon as Harry overheard that she was awake, he was grabbing for his coat and boots.

"I guess Harry would rather go home to meet the little girl, Mrs. Guptil, but thanks very much for offering to keep him."

Elizabeth buttoned him up and tied his scarf tightly, ready to head back with him to her own kitchen. "Thank you, Mrs. Guptil," she said, nudging Harry to speak.

"Thank you, Mrs. Guptil. Bye, Freddy," said Harry as he clutched his truck in his arms.

As soon as they were out the door, Harry was, as usual, full of questions, and talked her ear off all the way home.

"What's her name, Lizzie? Why did she land here? Did she talk to you? Does she like to play hide and seek? Do you think she'll play with me?"

"Harry, come on, no more questions. I can't answer the ones you asked if you don't keep still." He stopped for a moment. "Her name is Lucy and she's from Nova Scotia and she was sailing with her grandfather on the *Horton* and we didn't talk about playing."

"I bet she'll play with me. She'll have to be careful with my trucks, and we can play hide and seek. When can I see her, Lizzie? I want to see her" … and on and on he went. Elizabeth was glad to find a chore for him to do to keep him quiet.

Harry made many trips fetching kindling for the wood box while Elizabeth began to think about the dinner that needed to be prepared. The excitement was over for now and the regular daily chores took over once again. Elizabeth sat at the table with her face in her hands and tried to think about all that she must do.

Just then Thomas and Francis burst in the door. "We got a duck, Lizzie, a big one! Just look how fat he is. Why don't you pluck him for dinner?" They spoke on top of one another.

"I'm not plucking him. You boys and Papa can do that, and if you get it done quickly, we can probably have him for dinner tomorrow. Tonight we're going to have fish cakes."

The boys looked at each other in surprise, and Thomas looked like he was about to speak but thought better of it. It was clear they had heard the authority of her voice and had no doubt in their minds that Lizzie was now in charge!

CHAPTER FIFTEEN

She's In Charge

As she got into bed that night, Elizabeth saw that Lucy was sleeping soundly. Lucy was still living in the bedroom all day and had insisted that her food be brought to her on a tray at suppertime. She said that she did not like Elizabeth's fishcakes, but ate them with gusto.

Elizabeth had told Papa, "I don't think I should have to wait on her any longer, Papa. She can come downstairs, I'm sure."

"Just be patient with her a bit longer. She's been through a great ordeal," reasoned Papa.

"But, Papa, I'm tired of bringing her things and of emptying the pot when she can get herself down to the outhouse. I know she can," an angry Lizzie pouted.

"Lizzie, I think she can, too, but in many ways she seems terrified of being here with us. And she hasn't even seen the boys yet. We'll give her 'til tomorrow and then we'll insist. Okay? I've not had any word yet from anyone about her family. The Lighthouse Service is checking on it. Maybe they'll know something tomorrow." Elizabeth had just nodded her head and continued cleaning up from supper.

As she reviewed the day in her mind, she watched the light through her window and began to drift off to sleep. Suddenly, she noticed the lantern through her window again. It was moving toward her room. She got out of bed and walked to the window. She did not want to awaken Lucy.

She was not afraid of the proud, but kindly face she saw coming up to the window. He smiled at her, and his face looked peaceful, not worried, as it had been the first time she saw him. He stood at the window and looked at Lucy for what seemed like a long time. Then he once again blew a kiss to her and smiled at Elizabeth, turned around and disappeared into the night.

Elizabeth had not told Papa of his other visits; she had not told anyone, keeping this secret deep within her. Actually, it had not been too difficult to keep the secret since she had been so very busy. But now she felt she had to tell Papa. She went to Papa's room and found him reading in his big chair.

"Papa, something just happened and I don't know how to explain it to you," she said as she curled up in his lap and told her story.

"Do you think you saw a ghost?"

"I … I don't know if I did or not. It seemed quite real to me and it happened three times."

"That's true, and each time you were just falling in or out of sleep. Soooo, could it have been a kind of dream?"

"Maybe, but tonight I got up and went to the window to see him more clearly, and he looked at me and smiled. What do you think Papa?"

"There are many stories on the seas about such spirit sightings, Lizzie. I have never seen one myself, but I wouldn't say it couldn't happen. The explanations I've heard are many. It is said that the ghosts are souls who are fighting death because they are uncertain that they will go to heaven, souls who have unfinished business on earth and are struggling to take care of it, and souls who feel they have debts to repay or vengeance to carry out. It is said that these souls fight to stay on earth just a little longer. I suppose a person could say that Captain MacPherson was dedicated to his granddaughter and loved her so much that he couldn't leave until he knew she was either going with him or safe and well with someone who would care for her."

"I think that's it, Papa," said Elizabeth. "He wanted to be sure she was alive and would have a good home. I saw his face and that's just what he seemed to be saying. I don't think I dreamed it, Papa. I don't, but I could have, I guess. I could have, but I really don't think so, I …"

Her exhaustion overwhelmed her and she lost her last words.

*   *   *   *

Papa looked at her softly closed eyes. Putting his powerful arms underneath her slight frame, he carried her to her bed, where he slipped her under the covers next to Lucy.

He kissed her head and left the two girls to their dreams. As he turned to go, he noticed a lantern light outside the window and took two quick steps over to the windowsill. He did not think it possible, but he saw the lantern swinging in mid-air—as if waving to him. He searched the night to see if he could see anyone holding the lantern. He thought he saw a human outline, slightly lighter than the sky. It had a captain's hat on its head, but he could see no facial features.

He lifted his hand to the window and waved back, whispering under his breath, "Don't worry, we'll take care of her. Don't worry." He watched the outline and the lantern glow fade in the distance, and he went back to his room and fell deeply asleep.

*   *   *   *

Elizabeth thought it was about time for Lucy to take some responsibility. She had come down for breakfast with everyone else, so she did get fed this morning.

"Lucy, I have to make some fish chowder for dinner today and it takes all of my concentration to get it right. I need to have you go outside every ten or so minutes and check on Harry to see that he is staying out of trouble," said Elizabeth.

"He's your brother, not mine. I have no intention of watching him," Lucy said resolutely.

"You'd better do it if you want any dinner today. I will NOT feed you anything more than a biscuit and water if you don't start helping around here. Papa said we don't have to do anything more than keep you alive if you are not willing to work, and I intend to do no more than that if you don't start cooperating," replied Elizabeth.

"I hate you! Your father better hurry up and find my grandfather. I'm sick of all of you and I want to go home," yelled Lucy, as she put on her coat and went out the door to the yard.

In a minute, she came back in and said, "He's playing near the walkway to the boat launch. I told him and Freddy to hang on it and fall in," said Lucy, smirking.

"You better go back out and get them away from there. They are not to go near any of the cliffs, ever. Now get going," insisted Elizabeth.

Lucy slammed her feet on the floor as she grabbed her coat off the hook and went out again. Elizabeth could hear her screaming at the top of her lungs and she had to laugh.

"Harry, get away from there. If you drown, I'll starve to death." Harry and Freddy came scrambling from the rocks near the boat ramp. "Now stay where I can see you. I don't want to come out here again." Lucy slammed the door behind her and moved her reading to a chair near the window where she looked out every so often.

Elizabeth sighed. Well, I guess that is progress, she thought. I still wish Mother were here. Elizabeth worked all day at cooking and laundry, and didn't even get to most of the cleaning. On top of that, she had been trying very hard to keep up with her studies in order to take the high school entrance test when Francis did. Luckily it wasn't canning time.

She made the boys clean the fish and ducks. They were pretty good about taking off their dirty boots at the door. They did help with the dishes most of the time, and Papa did all he could to help, but taking care of a family of five—no, now six—was exhausting. If only Lucy would start to help. If only Lucy were a regular little girl and not a spoiled little princess. If only …

Elizabeth was sitting at the table cutting up the potatoes for the fish chowder. She thought she would put her head down for a minute and … then she jerked her head up just as she thought she was reaching a sound sleep.

"Lizzie, we got a cod on our longlines," yelled Thomas. "It is a great big one. Enough for some fried fish and some chowder, too. We thought the lines were empty and, you know, Papa won't let us go out past the safety lines in winter, but then I saw it taut and pulled and there he was. A beauty, huh?"

Elizabeth sat up with a start and was staring at Thomas and Francis's smiling faces. They carried one of the biggest codfish she had ever seen, and were struggling to hold it. Even Lucy was curious and peeked in from the living room to see.

"My grandfather caught bigger fish than that," she remarked, and went back to her reading.

"As if I care," yelled Thomas. Elizabeth gave him a dirty look.

"I just got her to help watch Harry this morning, so don't rock the boat!" she ordered.

"Where is Harry?" asked Francis. "Let's show him our fish." He turned and went back outside, calling, "Harry, Harry, come see our great big fish." He looked around the yard and all around the house, and then went to look around Freddy's house, too. He walked to the edge of the boat ramp and down toward the light and the outbuildings. "Harry, Freddy, come on, don't hide. We caught a great big fish. Come see. Harry … Freddy…"

Finally, Francis gave up. "Lizzie, I can't see those boys anywhere. We had better look for them. I'll go get Mrs. Guptil."

"No, Francis, Mrs. Guptil went with Papa to the mainland. Quick. We have to find them." Then she turned to Lucy. "This is all your fault, you lazy, spoiled girl. You'd better hope my brother is all right."

Lucy looked defiant. "I don't care if he is or not. I told you, he isn't my brother."

Francis had had enough of Lucy. Usually a silent young man, he walked into the living room and went right up to Lucy, curled up in a chair. He was tall for his age and he loomed over her.

He said, "Listen, little girl, this family rescued you from certain death and took care of you until you were well. You had better hope that our brother is alive and you'd better help us find him. Me and my brother and sister have had about all of you we can stomach. Now get your coat on and get searching."

Elizabeth and Thomas could hardly believe their ears, but there wasn't time for cheering. They were grabbing warm clothes and running out the door. "Haaarrrrry, Freeeeeedddy," everyone was yelling into the cold February air. Francis gave the search orders.

"Thomas, go out toward Summer Beach. Lizzie, to the berry

patches, ah … you go with her, Lucy. I'll take the cliff side. Whistle if you find them." Elizabeth pulled Lucy along with her. She ran out toward the center of the island, muttering as she ran.

"Stupid child. Stupid, stupid child," she said, not knowing whether she meant Lucy or Harry.

The berry patches were empty, so Elizabeth headed further down the east side of the island. As they ran toward the ocean, the skeleton of the *Horton* came into view. Lucy stopped running when she saw it. She gasped and stared at the ship. She had not seen it since she first arrived on Jib.

Elizabeth could see the shocked look on the little girl's face, and then a look of horror. All of the anger she had felt toward Lucy vanished as she watched the little girl look over the rubble before her. Elizabeth said, "Come on, Lucy, we'd better keep going till we find Harry." She took her arm and gently led the little girl away from the pieces of masts and hull, tables and capstans that littered the place. Lucy went with her, slowly at first, and then as fast as she could go.

They ran toward the cliffs on the other side of the island. As they neared them, they heard Francis calling again, "Harry, Freddy, Harry, Freddy." They met up and went up and down the shore calling for the boys. Soon they heard Thomas calling as well.

The wind was picking up and it was hard to hear much during the gusts. "What was that?" shouted Thomas. "I thought I heard someone yelling." They stopped and listened and heard a small voice in the distance. Everyone ran toward the sound coming from the edge of a crevice in the rocky cliffs. Francis motioned all the children to stay back as he went to look over the rocks to the surf below. He gasped at what he saw.

Harry and Freddy were huddled between two rocks about six feet below the edge of the cliff. They were alternately yelling and crying. Their small faces turned up when they heard Francis call to them. "Fred, Harry, hold on, hold on tight."

"Papa, Papa, I want my Papa," cried Freddy. "Help! Help!" The two shivering boys cried even louder.

"Thomas, run back and get a rope, and get Mr. Guptil," ordered Francis as he started to climb down toward the boys, he carefully chose his footholds on his way down. "Can you reach your hand up to me, Fred?" he asked.

"No, my foot is caught, can't, can't pull it out," Freddy cried. And Harry continued to cry with him as the waves of the incoming tide crashed around them and licked at their pant legs.

Mr. Guptil reached them in a matter of minutes.

"Papa, Papa," yelled Freddy.

"Francis, be careful," shouted Mr. Guptil. He took off his coat and tossed it down to Francis. "Wrap this around the boys," he said.

Francis draped it over a shivering Freddy and took off his own coat to wrap around Harry. The little boys were swimming in warm woolen coats.

"Can you free his foot, Francis?" called Mr. Guptil, as Francis worked the little foot gently back and forth. The rocks had held so tightly around his boot that he couldn't get his foot out of it. Francis unlaced the boot and carefully pulled on the small stocking foot. Gently he eased it out of the boot.

"There, I got it out. He's free," yelled Francis.

"I can see Papa coming toward Jib," shouted Thomas. "He'll be here in a few minutes. Hey, there's someone else in the boat."

"Never mind," said Mr. Guptil. "I'm going to throw one end of the rope down to you, Francis, and hold the other tight." He tied the rope around his waist and threw the end over the cliff.

"Got it," yelled Francis.

"Wrap it around under his arms. And tie a strong knot—a bow-line."

"Okay, he's all set," replied Francis, tugging on the rope to make sure it would hold. The little boys didn't weigh much, but it seemed like a lot when they were hanging over the cliff.

"You children pull gently when I tell you to," instructed Mr. Guptil. "Okay, now … easy, okay … a little more. There you are. … That's good, keep pulling." He backed up across the field at the top of the cliff while Francis lifted Freddy as high as he could so the others could pull him to the top. Freddy was silent as a hot summer day, a look of pure terror on his face as he rose to the top of the cliff. When he got to the edge, he grabbed it and scrambled over, dragging his throbbing leg. Elizabeth reached for him and gathered him into her arms..

"You're safe now, Freddy; you're okay." She soothed him as he shook from both cold and fear.

"Untie him and get that rope back down here," called Francis.

Thomas untied the rope and threw the end back to his brother, who tied it expertly around Harry. When he lifted Harry's arm to wrap the rope around his small torso, Harry screamed, "Oooowwww!"

"Oh, no, Harry, something wrong with your wing?" asked Francis as he saw Harry's arm flop to his side. "We'll get you fixed up soon," he said to Harry, and then yelled up to the others, "Okay pull 'im up, but take it easy. I think his arm is broken."

Harry's big, blue eyes opened wide while he watched the mighty waves crashing beneath him as he was suspended above them. His brother and sister and even Lucy were pulling him to safety, and his arm felt as if it weighed a hundred pounds as it hung at his side. Soon his sister was holding him as he sobbed into his brother's warm coat. Lucy watched as Elizabeth spoke softly to Harry to calm him and hugged him to warm him.

As soon as Francis reached the top of the cliff, Mr. Guptil picked up Freddy and headed for the houses. Francis lifted Harry carefully from Elizabeth's arms and followed him. As they reached the frozen dirt patch of the summer garden, their father and Mrs. Guptil caught up with them. The Guptils took Freddy to their house and the Bartons followed Papa to theirs. Harry was still wrapped in Francis's coat, holding on to Francis's neck with one arm.

CHAPTER SIXTEEN

Family

"Well, Harry, lucky this is only a little dislocated elbow. You've done this before, remember? Doc Stebbins taught me how to fix it, and only a few months ago we had to do it again. Why does this keep happening, Harry?"

Harry managed a weak grin as Papa quickly maneuvered the elbow to pop it back in place. It was a pretty painless procedure if it was done right, and Papa was good at it.

"There you are, good as new!"

Harry hugged his father tightly. He had stopped sobbing and stopped shaking. The children were gathered around watching Papa "work magic" on Harry's elbow.

"That's quite a neat trick," said a familiar voice behind the children. They all turned at once, and Harry peeked out of Francis's coat.

"Miss Honey!" They cheered in chorus. "Miss Honey, you're back!"

"I knew I saw someone else in the boat," added Thomas.

"Yes, I am back, and none too soon, I would think! You've been a bit unruly lately, I see!" She laughed. "But, all's well that ...."

"Ends well!" they chimed in, having learned this phrase from her during their lessons.

"Now, who is your new friend?" asked Miss Honey, knowing perfectly well that the little red head belonged to Lucy, as Elizabeth had described in her letters.

"Oh, that's Lucy," said Thomas. "She was supposed to be watching Harry when he climbed down the cliff."

"But my train fell down there and I had to get it. Papa made it for me and it was my favorite thing."

"Next time, Harry, go get some help from someone bigger than you, okay?"

"Okay, Miss Honey, I promise," replied Harry.

"But Thomas is right. Lucy was supposed to be watching," said Francis. "And I warned her about what would happen to her if anything happened to him." He walked menacingly toward Lucy, who did not know that Francis would never hurt her.

"Don't hit me!" she yelled as she cowered behind a nearby chair. "I'm sorry, I didn't mean to. I …" She collapsed into sobs.

"Francis, that will be enough," said Papa sternly, his eyes flashing at Francis. "Don't worry little one, Francis won't lay a hand on you.

Elizabeth went over to her father and whispered something into his ear.

"Miss Honey needs some help with her things, children. Please go to the boat and get them and take them to her room. Miss Honey, would you take Harry up to his bed for a nap? He's just about asleep now. Lucy, come over here and see me."

This last order was said very sternly. They recognized his serious tone. Lucy came to the kitchen table. Papa patted the chair seat next to him and Lucy slid up on it. Her eyes focused on the worn oilcloth covering the table. She did not look at Papa.

"One of the things I found waiting for me at the post office was a letter from your Great Aunt May."

Lucy's eyes widened, but she continued to stare at the table.

"She told me all about your parents' accident and about your grandmother being sick for so long before she died. She explained that your grandfather was all that you had left as she is bedridden and can't care for you. She sends her love to you, though, and hopes that you are well. I told her in my letter that you are welcome to stay with us if you wish, or you can choose to go back to Nova Scotia to the orphanage in Halifax. I will be writing to her as soon as I have your decision. You don't have to stay here, Lucy. But we'd be glad to have you. If you stay, however, you have to do as the other children do. Chores, responsibilities, schoolwork. That's all part of life on Jib. If you stay, it won't be as a guest, but as a full family member. I have to be able to trust you as I do the other children. You'll have to obey Mother and me as readily as they do. Take some time to think this over. I'd like your answer by breakfast tomorrow."

Lucy nodded, then looked at Papa. "You would still have me … even, even after what happened to Harry?"

"My children aren't perfect, Lucy. And I don't expect you will be, either. Knowin' when you've been wrong and bein' willin' to take responsibility, that's all I care about. Takin' care of each other is an important part of life here. Make sure you can promise to do your best. That's all I expect."

Lucy nodded, and while Papa got up to see how the children were getting on with his instructions, Lucy stayed at the table. Elizabeth came into the kitchen and began preparing for dinner.

"I guess we better put on a cold dinner, Lucy. It's too late to cook much."

"There's some chicken broth left from Sunday. That would be good for Harry. I'll get it and heat it up," said Lucy.

"Okay. The rest of us can have biscuits and cheese with some cold, smoked herring."

They worked side by side for a while, and then Lucy shyly approached Elizabeth.

"If you still want me to be your sister, Elizabeth, I'm willing to behave myself. I know I've been awful. My grandfather did spoil me, but he also taught me good manners and good behavior. He would be very disappointed in me today. I've been … I'm sorry."

"I do want you, Lucy. You don't know how much I've wanted a sister. When you were sleeping after the shipwreck, I wished so hard that you would live and be my sister. Then when you woke up and were … ah, well, you were so awful."

"I know, I know. I have a terrible temper. I just thought if I insisted loudly enough, my grandfather would come back for me. But today I realized that he won't be coming and I never got to say goodbye." Lucy looked longingly out the window.

"It must have been a shock to see the boat. I was shocked myself. It was so empty out there." Elizabeth thought about the captain's goodbye to Lucy, and although she was tempted to blurt it out, she vowed in her heart to tell Lucy about it someday. Lucy began to sob and Elizabeth reached over and pulled her into her apron-covered body with long, graceful arms. She stroked her red hair and embraced her—it was the only embrace Lucy had had for some time. Elizabeth had nothing more to say, but only held Lucy and gave her time to sob.

Papa came into the kitchen looking for his dinner. The girls had laid out all they had and it was not a feast.

Lucy approached Papa tentatively. "I don't need to wait until to-morrow," she said to him. "I know that I want to stay here, Mr. Barton, if you will have me. I know that I can be a much better girl and that I can make my grandfather proud of me."

Papa picked her up and gave her a big hug. "Then, Lucy, you must call me Papa, like the others. And, you must begin taking a turn with all the chores. Do you agree?"

"I do …. ah … Papa, I do!" she replied.

"Okay. Now you must know that Lizzie is very good at forgiving, but the boys will be much harder to win over. So don't expect them to be very fond of you right away."

"I know. It was so terrible, what happened to Harry, wasn't it? But, I made Harry some broth for dinner."

Papa looked at the little redhead with her freckles standing out on her face and fell into a deep, belly laugh. "You've made a good start, a very good start."

"Mr. B … I mean, Papa, do you think we could have a funeral for my grandfather? I know now that he is dead and will never come back for me. Do you think you could read some scripture and say some things over at the shipwreck? Grandfather did that once on the ship for a sailor who went overboard in the night during a storm. It was nice. We all said goodbye to him. And I threw some flower petals into the water."

"I think that is a very good idea. We will do it tonight after supper," said Papa. "Now, let's eat!"

The older boys came running to the kitchen at the sound of the word "eat." Miss Honey came downstairs and said that Harry was sleeping peacefully.

"I'll take him some broth in a little while," said Lucy. Francis and Thomas were astonished.

"Don't put anything bad in it, Lucy," said Thomas.

"Thomas," said Papa, "you read too many mysteries! Lucy would do no such thing." Both boys looked at Lucy very suspiciously. But Papa said no more and everyone ate.

"Tonight, after supper, we are going to have a funeral service for Captain MacPherson and his crew down at the shipwreck. Francis and Thomas, get all the lanterns together and make sure they have candles. Miss Honey, would you please find some scripture to read. Lucy and I will work on the eulogy." The children were speechless but nodded in agreement.

*   *   *   *

At six o'clock the children followed Papa out past the garden and toward the Summer Beach. As they passed the berry patch and climbed the gently sloping rocks at the center of the island, they could see the remains of the *Horton*. It was the first time Harry had seen the ship close up and he held tightly to Miss Honey's hand. They walked in silence. Papa held firmly to Lucy's hand and led her to the cliff overlooking the ship. The ocean crashed loudly and thunderously on the beach, and the sun was just above the horizon to the west. Papa gathered the little group and began the service. He removed his cap and the boys followed his example. He put Lucy in front of Elizabeth and put his hands on her shoulders, and then he said:

"Let us pray. Dear Lord, we have come here tonight to willingly give over to you the care of this grandfather, Captain Isaiah MacPherson, known on earth to be a good and honest man. We are glad that he will be with you in heaven and we ask that you will bless us as we travel on in this life without his earthly love and guidance. We pray especially for Lucy, that she can hold the memories of him in her heart, and, as she feels able, that she can share her knowledge of this man with us so that we can know more about him and understand her great love for him."

Then Miss Honey read from the Bible.

"The Lord is my shepherd, I shall not want …"

Lucy spoke next, in a very quiet voice.

"My grandfather was a very fine ship's captain. He loved the *Horton* with all his heart and he took very good care of her. He was a good captain to his crew, and they liked him. But the best thing he did was to be a grandfather. When my grandmother died, he would not leave me with strangers or in the orphanage, even though his friends thought he should. He said to me, 'Lucy, we are all that is left of this family and we are going to be together.' On the ship he taught me my lessons, read to me from the Bible, and taught me things kids don't learn in school, like reading ocean charts and navigating with a sextant. He taught me to treat the crew well and to have good manners. I am going to try to remember forever all the things he taught me and make him proud of me."

As brave as Lucy tried to be, she couldn't help breaking down into sobs. Papa picked her up and held her to his shoulder.

"We commend thy servant Isaiah MacPherson to thee, O Lord. Remember us in our sorrow. Amen." Then he carried Lucy back across the rocks toward the house. It was darker now and the children had their lanterns lit. Elizabeth was at the end of the line with Miss Honey. She watched the twinkling of the lanterns ahead of her. Then she looked out to the ocean, searching for some sign of the captain. But there was nothing, only the darkening sky and the wailing wind and the pounding of the surf.

CHAPTER SEVENTEEN

Daisy

The letter from Nana was a great treat for Elizabeth; she read it and re-read it. At night she folded it up and put it back into the envelope and tucked it under her pillow.

"You'll get to know my Nana," she said to Lucy. "She can make anything and she can sing more songs than you knew there were. She can put up more vegetables, make more jam, and she makes the best bread ever. Mother's is good, too, but Nana's is the best. She's coming again in the spring. When the baby comes home she'll be here to help."

"When is that baby coming home, Lizzie?" asked Lucy.

"After she's born, silly, and Mother is well enough to travel. That is, if everything goes right. I say extra prayers every night for Mother and the baby."

"You said 'she,' Lizzie. I thought we don't know about babies until they are born."

"Most people don't, Lucy, but I'm wishing this one to be a girl so hard, she just can't be anything else."

Lucy laughed. "That's silly, Lizzie. It won't work."

"It's just got to, Lucy. It has got to."

After their prayers, the two girls fell off to sleep. The next day, they woke up to sunshine and puffy clouds. Papa had let them all sleep and it was past nine when they got down to the kitchen. Miss Honey was there with Harry, who was looking better than he had yesterday. His arm was better, too, as they could see, for Harry was busy teasing Scat with a piece of paper tied to a string. Up and down his arm went to make the paper jump this way and that, as the cat tried to pounce on it.

Slam! Scat threw her whole body toward the paper and hit the bare kitchen floor while the paper skittered away and Harry laughed a great belly laugh.

The jingle of the telephone startled everyone. It rang so infrequently on Jib because it was just for emergencies.

"The baby!" shouted Elizabeth staring at the phone. "The baby was born!" and she picked up the receiver.

"Elizabeth, is that you?"

"Yes," Elizabeth answered, surprised at the voice on the other end of the phone.

"This is Aunt Sally. Is your father there?"

"He's out at the light," Elizabeth replied. "I'll get him." She ran quickly out the back door, across the porch, down the stairs and across the grass to the light. Papa came back at a run and, huffing and puffing a bit, picked up the phone.

"Yes, Sally. What is it?" he said in a worried tone of voice, for Aunt Sally, Papa's sister who lived in Boston with Nana, rarely called Jib. He gave the children a signal to go to the living room, out of earshot, and when he thought they were safely out of the room he turned his attention to the phone call.

"Mother is very ill. She has picked up the influenza, probably from me; she is not doing well, at all. I think you should come."

"It must be bad, then," Papa replied. "I want to come, Sally, but I don't think I should. It would be terrible if I were to bring sickness to these children. I read in the paper just yesterday that the old ones and the young ones are dying from it. I'm sorry, Sally. But I better stay here and tend the children."

"You're right, Will. That was selfish of me. What was I thinking? I am just worried … and scared," replied Aunt Sally. "The doctor was just here, and he said he didn't think she would make it. She's very strong and fighting hard, but this is a fierce disease and it is even taking some of the strongest down. Mr. Thomas, the baker, and his son are very sick and the baker's wife, as hearty as any woman I know, has died."

"We will pray, Sally," said Papa. "That's all we can do. You take care that you don't get sick. Our mother wouldn't have anyone else."

"I think I was the one who gave it to her. I had a very mild case, though; I thought it was just a cold, and then a day or so later, Mother came down with it. I know it was my fault."

"Don't think that, Sally. She might have gotten it from the delivery boy or the postman just as easily. Try not to blame yourself. Even if you did give it to her, it wasn't on purpose. You can't help what happened."

"I guess you're right, Will. Wish you could be here, but I'll do my best. I'll call if things change. Bye, Will."

"Bye, Sally," said Papa.

Elizabeth had stayed close enough to hear bits and pieces of Papa's side of the conversation, and her face had turned white as she realized someone was sick.

Not Nana, she thought. *I just got her letter. She's fine. Aunt Sally is the sick one. Nana is fine. She's fine.*

Papa called the girls back to the kitchen.

"Nana has a bad case of the influenza," he said. "She might not make it. Let us pray for her." He took their hands in his and prayed, but all Elizabeth could hear pounding in her brain was the word *"NO! NO, NO, NO, NO, NOOOOO!" This cannot be happening. This must not be happening. I know what it is to lose someone. I remember Jenny's little limp body. No, not Nana. It can't be.*

The day wore on and on and into the evening, the children remaining quiet, each lost in his or her own thoughts. At the supper table Miss Honey tried to cheer them up a bit.

"Here is some lovely, fricasseed duck from that last, nice, fat one Francis got. Look at the lovely big pieces of meat in this. And I learned this potato casserole recipe out at White Head from Mrs. Carey, who is the most wonderful cook."

On and on she went with cheerful talk, until she saw Papa's face. He was giving her a look that told her it was no use to try to distract them. They were all too concerned about Nana.

Harry picked at his dinner with his fork, and Francis could only eat half of his. Thomas started asking questions. "When do you think Aunt Sally will call again, Pa? Maybe we should call her. Maybe the doctor found some good medicine and she's much better and Aunt Sally just forgot to let us know."

"Thomas, eat your supper. Aunt Sally will call when she can," said Papa.

Elizabeth drank her milk and nibbled at a biscuit. After the dishes were done, she picked up a book, read a few pages, and put it down again. As darkness fell, she looked out the window at the light and thought about the talk she'd had with Nana about dying.

None of the other adults ever talked about dying, but with Nana she talked about everything, even the things no one talked about. And they wrote letters to each other all the time. She had written to Nana about her pictures of the sailors swimming forever in the blue-green waters off Barbados. That's where her grandfather Barton was; she was sure.

Nana had written back, "No one really knows what heaven is like, Elizabeth. So your picture of it is as good as anyone's. I believe God takes us to a beautiful, wonderful place, and if you think that is warm waters that are blue and green, then that's just fine. My husband, your grandfather, would like a place like that, I know he would."

I bet Nana would like it there as well, she thought, picturing Nana swimming around with the bright-colored fish in her black coat and hat and carrying her pocketbook. The thought brought a slight smile to her lips. Then she thought about life here on Jib without Nana. *She can't go yet. Not now. I need her here. Mother needs her when the baby comes.* She fell into a fitful sleep in the chair by the living room window, and Papa carried her up to bed. Lucy was fast asleep, and the rest of the house was as silent as could be.

The ringing started in her dream. She could see the telephone but could not reach it. It was too high off the ground and she was very, very small. But it kept ringing and ringing.

"Lizzie, Lizzie!" yelled Lucy. "The telephone is ringing and no one is answering it." It was barely dawn. Papa must be out at the light already and no one else was up, or else the boys had already gone hunting.

"Lucy, run and get Papa while I answer it." Lucy and Elizabeth threw off the covers and jumped onto the icy floor, both with bare feet. The shock of the cold outside the bedcovers helped to wake them up and they slid quickly down the hall to the stairs, taking them two at a time. Lucy grabbed her coat and went out the door, still barefoot. The telephone was still ringing.

"Hello, Jib Island," she answered. "This is Elizabeth Barton speaking." The voice on the other end sounded very far away and very quiet.

"Good morning, Elizabeth Barton, this is Hildy Barton speaking."

"Mother, oh, Mother." Elizabeth began to cry.

"I miss you, too, my girl, I really do. Is your Papa there?"

"Lucy just went to get him," she answered, breathing hard. "How are you, Mother? How are you?"

"I am fine, but tired. This little sister of yours has been very hungry and awake for hours, it seems."

"A sister? Really? It is a sister?" Just then Papa came through the door and Elizabeth handed him the telephone. "I have a sister, Papa, a sister!"

"Hildy?" Papa said, huffing and puffing into the phone. "Are you all right? And the baby? … All right? You don't say. … Well, that's just fine, Hildy, just fine. I'll tell the children. You rest now. Give her a kiss for me."

"What did she say, Papa, what?" asked Elizabeth, jumping up and down on the kitchen floor.

"She's fine and the baby is fine. She has reddish hair and blue eyes, but other than that, she looks exactly like you did, Elizabeth. She has five fingers on each hand and five toes on each foot and she is perfect. Thanks be to God!"

"Lucy, we have a perfect sister!" said Elizabeth. Lucy looked surprised.

"You were right, Lizzie. How did you know?" Then the expression on her face changed. "Can she really be my sister, too?" she asked.

"If you promise to help me take care of her!" said Elizabeth.

"I promise, I promise!" shouted Lucy, as she skipped into the living room and went round and round, saying, "We have a sister, we have a sister!"

Breakfast was a happy event, celebrated with pancakes made by Elizabeth and Lucy. Although no one had forgotten about Nana, they were very excited about the new baby, who would be coming home, and they were hungry because no one had eaten much at supper the night before. The older boys had been successful in trapping several lobsters, which would become dinner.

Harry, wound up because his last meal had been so slight, shoveled pancakes into his mouth and talked at the same time. "I did say I wanted a brother, but a sister will be okay, too, 'cause I will be the big brother and take care of her and teach her not to go near the edge of the cliff."

Laughter erupted at the table.

Thomas proudly finished a stack of eight pancakes and took more than his share of blueberry syrup. Elizabeth and Lucy could hardly keep up with the requests for more pancakes.

"Elizabeth," said Papa, "Mother said that, because you wanted a sister so very much, you may give her a name."

"Me? Name the baby? Wow!" replied Elizabeth.

"Why don' we name it 'Sam'?" asked Harry. "That's what I would name her."

"Sam is a boy's name, Harry," answered Thomas.

"Yup, if we name it Sam, then it will be a boy, not a girl," said Harry very seriously. Even Papa laughed at that, while Francis tousled Harry's hair and said, "Good try, Harry, but it won't work."

Then the ringing of the phone interrupted life at Jib for the third time in two days. Papa took a deep breath and got up from his chair and walked to the phone. The eyes of all the children followed him and were glued to his face as he answered.

"Jib Island, Will Barton speaking. Hullo, Sally. Yes, I thought so. I will tell the children and call you back soon."

The children had silently gathered around their father, reaching their arms around him and each other. He picked Harry up and let the others cling to him for what seemed like a whole morning. No one cried or spoke. They had cried most of yesterday, and today they found comfort in silence. Eventually, Papa put Harry down and hugged each of the children.

"I have to tell your mother. You children go wait in the living room. All of this news in one day . . . 'tis a bit much."

"Papa?" said Elizabeth.

"Yes, Lizzie," replied her father, turning back from the phone.

"Tell Mother, tell her . . . that the baby's name is going to be . . . is . . . Daisy."

Papa nodded. "Of course, after Nana," he said, " of course." He caressed Elizabeth's upturned face with his worn hand and leaned down and put a kiss gently on her forehead. He returned to the telephone, and soon the children heard him speaking in hushed words into the receiver. He spoke longer than they had ever heard him speak on the phone to anyone. When he finished, he said goodbye to the children and went back outside to the light. Elizabeth watched him walking a slow—no, very slow—pace, and saw him disappear through the door at the bottom of the lighthouse, his head bent and his hair flying in the wind.

*   *   *   *

Papa and Mother decided that it would not be possible for any of them to travel to Boston to help Aunt Sally prepare a small funeral for Nana. They had so much to care for at Jib and many preparations for bringing the new baby home.

Papa told the children, "We can't go to Boston for Nana's funeral. It would be very expensive and, because of the influenza, I can't take the chance of going myself and bringing the sickness back to Jib. Next week, when I bring Mother and Daisy home, we'll have a little service of our own, just like the one we had for Lucy's grandfather. You can all write something to say about your grandmother, if you like."

"Papa, where will we have the service?" asked Thomas.

"I don't know. Where do you children think we should have it?"

"She loved the raspberries," said Elizabeth.

"And she helped us plant them, remember?" said Francis.

"Then we will go out to the raspberry patch that she helped us plant and have the service there," said Papa.

Elizabeth went up to her bedroom and Lucy followed her.

"Lucy, I'd like to be by myself for a while," said Elizabeth. Lucy nodded and went back downstairs. Elizabeth went to the window and looked at the light and then out to the ocean. It was then that she noticed the ache in her stomach, and tears filled her eyes and spilled over onto her cheeks, dripping down to her pinafore. At first, her sobs were quiet, and then she held on to the window casing as her cries became great wails and her body shook from them. When she realized how loud they were, she tried to quiet down, but she couldn't do it. Her legs became weak and she lowered herself to the floor and shook with the great sobbing and sucking in of her breath. Her head began to throb and her eyes stung from what felt like quarts of tears running from them. Finally, no more tears could come and the sobs slowly subsided to small, shaking whimpers. For now she was done, but she would cry again and again, every time she felt the huge hole in her belly.

"We never really lose the people we love who die," Nana had said. "They live in us and in all the wonderful things we remember. I can remember your grandfather so vividly in his handsome captain's uniform the day we married. Every time I do something he taught me, I remember him. I can see him holding your father the day they first met. Your father was three months old and your grandfather had been out at sea when he was born. The look of love in his eyes was something I will never forget."

And then Elizabeth said out loud, as she sat alone in her room, "You will live in me forever, Nana. I will remember everything we did and everything we talked about. You will never leave me, but I will miss you terribly, every day. And I will teach little Daisy what you taught me, and why her name is the best name in the whole world."

CHAPTER EIGHTEEN

The Decision

Papa came in from the lighthouse, hung his jacket on the hook in the hallway, and stepped into the kitchen. Daisy was busily feeding in Mother's lap, and he smiled as he heard her smack, smack, smacking as she nursed.

"You are a noisy little thing," he said as he brushed his rough fingers across the wisps of reddish hair sticking straight up from Daisy's head, and then rested his hand on Mother's shoulder and gave a little squeeze.

"Hildy," Papa said, "I think the seas have calmed enough from these blasted winds. I'm going to the mainland to get the new parts for the donkey engine. They're waitin' for me at Nick's garage. D'you have a list for the store?"

"'Course," she replied, "and a Sears and Roebuck order in at the post office."

At the mention of the post office, Elizabeth's ears pricked up.

"You're goin' to get the mail, too, right?" she asked.

"Sure," said Papa.

"Well, can I go and help you?"

Papa tried to conceal a smile. "If Mother can do without you, I guess."

Elizabeth looked over to see Mother nod. The help Elizabeth gave her each day with the housework and the baby made her daughter more than deserving of a treat.

"Can Lucy come, too?"

"I guess," said Mother. "It can be a girls' trip."

"Except for little Daisy," said Elizabeth, as she dried her hands, and then walked over to Daisy, who had finished nursing. She reached down and took her sister from her Mother's arms, carefully cradling her tiny head. Just then Daisy produced a great "BURRPPP."

"My goodness, Daisy, that noise was a lot bigger than you are," said Elizabeth. She kissed the little head as she placed Daisy in her "kitchen basket," a wicker laundry basket tucked between Mother's locker and the dish cupboard. Elizabeth, while waiting for Daisy to come home from the mainland, had woven the pink ribbons through the wicker, tying them into bows at each end. It was the same basket in which all of the children had spent their first few months, except Francis, who had spent only a month because he grew very long, very quickly.

"Better get your coat, Lizzie. I'm leaving now," said Papa.

"I'm comin'," she said as she kissed her mother's cheek, grabbed her coat from the hook in the hall, and followed Papa out the door. She pulled on her coat as she ran to the garden where Lucy was busy planting some flower seeds. "C'mon Lucy, we can go to the mainland with Papa." Lucy didn't hesitate; she dropped her hoe and followed Elizabeth to the boathouse at a dead run.

The seas were choppy but not wild. They were gray under a partly cloudy sky, and Elizabeth enjoyed the roar of the engine, which prevented conversation. As she had hundreds of times before, she watched the buildings on the shore grow larger and larger. She noticed the first people she could see or the first horse or dog. She looked for something new or unusual. This morning she saw a whole group of children hanging over the pier with fishing lines. *School is out for the summer, I guess*, she thought to herself. She didn't feel quite the longing or envy that she used to feel when seeing groups of children at play. She had Lucy now and, of course, they both had Daisy. Even with two new sisters in one year, she was eager to learn whether she would be allowed to go off of Jib to high school. She noticed the knots in her stomach as she thought of getting the letter.

Lucy and Elizabeth scrambled up the ladder to the pier and ran ahead of Papa up to the store. The store bell gave its familiar ring when the girls pushed the heavy plank door open. Papa followed them to the post office counter, where Elizabeth stood at the window. "Good morning, Mrs. Wallace," she said, and then couldn't say anymore.

Mrs. Wallace looked puzzled. "Elizabeth, why so quiet today? You're always so chatty. Cat got your tongue?"

Elizabeth still couldn't speak. Papa asked Mrs. Wallace for the mail. She found the Bartons' box and pulled out some letters. "Quite a bit today, Will. One for Francis and even one for Elizabeth," she said, as her eyes crinkled up in a smile.

Papa looked through the pile. "I think the one from the school district is what you're hopin' for. Right, Elizabeth?"

"It's that time o' year. Quite a few came in. Catharine Mett, over to Islesboro, just got hers this morning. Goin' to Bar Harbor next year. Why, seems only yesterday you and Catharine could barely see over the counter." Mrs. Wallace kept talking, but Elizabeth wasn't listening. She was only looking at the long, white envelope that Papa had put into her hands. She took it outside the store and sat on the bench with Lucy right on her heels.

"What's it say, Elizabeth? Did you pass? Are you going? C'mon, open it, open it."

Elizabeth sat for another minute, staring at the address typed on the front.

Elizabeth Barton
Jib Island, Maine

She hesitated a moment longer, gave a long sigh, and opened the letter. The paper had only a few words on it.

Elizabeth Barton 82% Pass
Jib Island, Maine
Assigned to Bar Harbor

Lucy read it over Elizabeth's shoulder. "You did it! You did it! Hurray for you, Elizabeth." Then, turning to Papa who was just coming out of the store, Lucy yelled, "She passed. She passed."

"'Spected she would. She's a smart girl," Papa said with a broad smile. He came over to look at the letter. "Bar Harbor, eh? That's a big school. They oughta be able to keep up with you. That's my girl," he said as he patted her shoulder and winked at her. Elizabeth smiled back, but was very quiet.

Papa said, "Let's walk up to the garage and get my parts, and then come back and pick up the packages here, and maybe get a little penny candy to celebrate." The girls went along with Papa, Lucy skipping around Elizabeth, who was quiet and not at all as excited as Papa had expected she would be.

"What's wrong, Lizzie?" he asked.

"Nothin'."

"I would have thought you'd be jumpin' outa your skin. I said you could go if you passed, and you passed. So I guess you're goin'."

"Yup, I guess I am," said Elizabeth.

The little group reached the garage, got Papa's parts, and headed back toward the store. The girls chose their candy, picked out some for the boys, and headed back to the pier carrying their packages. Elizabeth had put her letter in Papa's pocket. As they headed out to Jib, Elizabeth watched the lighthouse grow taller and taller. She searched the island for her family and finally saw Francis and Thomas heading toward the Keeper's House carrying some seabirds they had shot.

Thomas and Francis saw them coming in and waited at the boathouse to give a hand in hauling the boat up on the skids.

"She passed! She did it!" shouted Lucy to the boys.

"Ssshhhh," said Elizabeth, glaring at Lucy. "I'll tell them when I'm ready. It's my letter." Lucy pouted and slouched back into the boat.

As soon as the boat was properly stored, the Sears packages, groceries, and mail taken to Mother, and the parts for the engine taken to the light, Papa took Francis's letter out of his pocket and handed it to him when none of the others were watching.

"Why don't you open this, son? You might as well know," said Papa. Francis nodded and took the envelope, opening it slowly and reading it quickly.

Francis Barton 80% Pass
Jib Island
Assigned to Bar Harbor

"I passed . . . but Pa, I don't want to go," Francis pleaded.

Papa put his hand on Francis's shoulder. "Son, we've had this talk before. You have t'get your high school education. I know it sounds like a great punishment, but it really isn't; your world's goin' to be very different from mine. I can see that my children are goin' to need a different kind of education than the one I had, and you'll have a chance to do things I could never do. The Lighthouse Service is already making new requirements for keepers, so even if you want to be a keeper, you'll need more education than I had. The world seems to be changin' a lot since the war. Accept it, Son. You do have to go. It'll be okay, Francis. You'll come home often and we'll come when we can. Both you and Elizabeth will be livin' with Young Arch and his wife, Ethel. They live close to the school so you can walk back and forth."

"Guess I hafta." Francis hung his head and walked away, absorbed in his own thoughts as his father walked to the house to get ready for supper.

At supper, Francis announced that he had passed and would be going to high school in Bar Harbor. Mother looked very pleased and the other children cheered for him. Elizabeth was next.

"I passed and I'll be going to Bar Harbor with Francis." Again everyone cheered, and lively talk filled the kitchen about the plans for sending two children off to high school.

"Thomas, you'll become the eldest when the others go," said Papa, "which means you'll have to do all the chores."

Thomas looked at Papa with great horror on his face, and then a mischievous expression came over his face. "No, I think we'll have to train Lucy and Harry," he said.

"Hey, c'mon," said Lucy, "I just learned how to do my own chores, and that's enough for now. Besides, I'm going to be helping to take care of Daisy."

"That's true," said Mother. Elizabeth's face fell as she thought about Lucy taking care of Daisy.

After supper, Elizabeth helped Mother clean up the kitchen. Lucy washed the dishes and Elizabeth dried them. "Daisy doesn't like to be burped on your shoulder, Lucy. Lay her across your lap. And she likes to sleep on her tummy, not on her back. Make sure her blankets are wrapped tightly so she doesn't kick them off and get cold." She went on and on with instructions.

At bedtime, Elizabeth saw that Lucy was asleep the minute she hit the pillow. She crept downstairs and found her father reading in his chair. Mother had gone to bed already.

"What is it, Lizzie?" he asked.

Elizabeth threw her arms around his neck from behind the chair and sighed.

"That was a big sigh."

"Papa, do I have to go to Bar Harbor this year, just 'cause I passed?"

"I don't think so, but you wanted to go so badly, Lizzie. What's this change of heart?"

"I just don't think I'm ready yet. I just got the sisters I always want-ed and now I am going to leave them. I don't want to. I want to stay and be with Daisy for a while and make sure Lucy knows what to do when I am gone. What would you think if I wanted to stay, Papa, just one more year? I could study here with Miss Honey and help tutor Thomas and Harry and Lucy. What d'ya think?"

"Letting you stay is no problem for me or your mother. We'll both be glad to have you here for another year. You're a smart girl, Lizzie. Not just in book learning, but in knowing about yourself. And that is even more important in this world. Knowing yourself can help you make good choices all the rest of your life. I'm proud of you, Lizzie. And I'm happy to have my girl next to me for a while longer. But it's your deci-sion, and I know you have a lot to think about, because you have so many plans and your studying is part of those plans. You need to think about what you might be giving up."

Elizabeth snuggled closer to her father and stroked his cheek with her hand. "I'll think about it more before I decide."

"Lots of hard decisions in life, Lizzie. Ya might as well get started learnin' how to make them!"

CHAPTER NINETEEN

Growing Up

"I do think that fall is the most beautiful season in Maine," said Miss Honey, as she looked out the schoolroom window toward the mainland and saw tinges of yellow on the trees by the shore. "You will love the bright colors of the leaves on the mainland in the fall, Francis. When I travel from island to island in the fall, I usually get a day or two in between on the mainland. It is still warm in the daytime, but crisp at night. You can pick apples from the trees and when you bite into them, they go 'crack' in your mouth instead of 'moosh,' the way they do when we take them out of the barrel in November or February on Jib. I guess there will be lots of things about the mainland that you will discover and like. Who knows, you might even find a girl or two you like."

Francis looked at Miss Honey in horror. This boy of few words was speechless. It had not occurred to him that he would be meeting girls at the high school. Unlike his sister, he had never longed for friendships.

Miss Honey sensed his apprehension and continued. "There will be boys, too, and you will certainly meet several who like to hunt and fish as you do. Don't worry, Francis, it will be fine at the high school. You don't think you are ready for this, but you are. It's time for a little adventure."

"I have adventure every day here on Jib, Miss Honey. Can't imagine I'll find any more someplace else."

"Just be open to it, Francis, just be open. And don't be surprised when it happens. Here are the books I think you should take with you," she said. She wished she could do something to help, but she knew that he'd have to find his own way.

"Thanks," said Francis as he left the schoolroom, his head and shoulders still drooping, and headed for his room to pack.

Mother came in as Francis was putting the final items in his suitcase. He looked around to see if he had forgotten anything.

"Did you put in that extra sweater, Francis?" asked Mother, bouncing a fussy, teething Daisy on her shoulder.

"Let me take her, Mother," said Elizabeth, who always wanted a chance to hold her sister.

Mother handed the baby over and continued to ask about sweaters and socks and hats and gloves.

"I put some letter paper and stamped envelopes in the supplies box, so make sure you write to us every week. Your father said he will bring you home for the weekend in October when the hunting is best. And Arch said he'd take you deer hunting in November, as well. He has a hunting rifle for you to use, so we are not sending yours."

"Yes, Mother," said Francis, who knew that she was just trying to cheer him up.

"Elizabeth, give Daisy to Lucy and go check that we got all the bundles from the attic. I don't want anyone to say my children weren't well supplied for school."

Thomas came running in the door. "Papa said for all of you to get going. He doesn't want to come back too late. Hurry up!" he yelled.

Harry was trying to carry Scat out to watch the leave taking, but could not get any cooperation from the cat. "C'mon, Francis will want you there to say goodbye. Ooouch . . . Mother, Scat scratched me for no reason." Harry scrambled out from under the table and ran off to find some sympathy.

Miss Honey came down from the schoolroom, dressed in her coat and carrying a small wrapped package.

"What's that?" asked Harry.

"It's a little going-away gift for Francis," she answered.

"What is it?" asked Harry.

"I guess you'll know when Francis knows. It's his and he can tell you or not tell you, as he wishes."

"I hope he wishes," said Harry.

Finally the bags were all packed and sitting in the hallway. Elizabeth instructed Lucy, "Get Daisy's hat on and wrap her up in her blanket so she can go out to say goodbye."

She took the stairs two at a time, and looked around for any bundles or suitcases in the hallway. She looked out of Francis's room to the boathouse and saw the guv'ment boat already laden with boxes. Miss Honey was standing by the boathouse in her hat and coat. Papa would do errands while he was on the mainland, and Miss Honey, after spending the summer, was going home to help out her mother. She would be back in a couple of months to work with the younger children. Harry was standing next to Miss Honey, wiping his eyes, as he had been crying all morning about her leaving.

Elizabeth flew down the stairs, grabbed her coat from the hook in the hall, and ran through the living room, where she saw Francis staring at his suitcase. She took a small package out of her pocket and walked over to Francis. She had wrapped it and put it in her pocket yesterday, because she had not wanted to forget it. Francis was still in the living room looking over his bags and deep in thought.

"Don't worry, Francis. Really. I don't think it will be at all like you think. Here, I made you some cookies and bought you an inkwell. I know you will be just fine. Write and tell me what it is like."

"I can't believe you don't want to come with me," said Francis. "You had the chance and everything. You've wanted this forever, Lizzie. Why don't you come? It's not too late."

"Oh, I do want to go off to school; I want to go very much. But I want this last year home on Jib, with Daisy and Lucy, especially; I want it more than I want to go off to school. And I have time to do both. It'll be next year before you know it and I'll be coming, too." She smiled broadly at her brother. "And then you'll wish I hadn't come!"

"I wish I thought the year would pass that quickly. For me it will seem like ten years, I bet." Francis laughed at that. "I will write, Lizzie, and you write, too."

"I promise, Francis."

They walked slowly toward the boathouse. Elizabeth carried one of Francis's boxes, and Francis carried everything else in his strong arms. He looked over Jib, out toward the berry patches, and could see that they were beginning to look like they did every fall—the leaves touched with a bit of brown and the raspberry canes beginning to dry. He looked back toward the light and at the Keeper's House, so perfectly white and proud, perched on this rock in the middle of the sea. How strong it looked to him, how safe. He stood for a moment, taking it all in, as if he might never return.

"Hey, Francis, let's go," shouted Papa. Francis took a very deep breath and then went over to his mother and kissed her goodbye. He reached down to little Daisy and kissed her, too. Then he patted Lucy firmly on her head.

"You better take care of my sister, and Harry, too, if you know what's good for you," he said with an impish grin.

"Our sister, Francis," Lucy corrected him. "Bye—hope it's not too bad!"

"Francis, bring me some candy when you come home," yelled Harry.

"Yeah, and see if Arch will let you borrow that great duck gun— just for the weekend so I can try it," added Thomas.

"Never mind, Thomas. Get in, Francis, you're holding up the whole works here," yelled Papa.

"Want to change your mind, Lizzie? I'll wait a couple minutes for you!" Papa teased.

"No thanks," said Elizabeth. She had taken Daisy back from Lucy and was bouncing her up and down. "But you can take me next year!"

They watched the boat go down into the gentle waves. It was a perfect day for a trip to the mainland. The sun was bright. The sea was quiet, stirring up just a bit of foam where only two days ago there had been great splashes of surf. All of them waved, Mother with tears in her eyes. Elizabeth took Daisy's tiny hand and waved it toward the boat. Lucy, who had gotten used to Francis's teasing, yelled, "Watch out, Francis, I think I see a hole in the boat!"

And Thomas yelled, "Remember to borrow the duck gun, Francis."

"Hush, Thomas," said Mother. "Really, Thomas, ask him to bring you some books!"

The boat became smaller and smaller as it sped toward the mainland and danced on the waves, until it looked as tiny as Daisy's hand bouncing in the soft Jib breeze. Elizabeth looked at her sister's little face and her sweet little mouth, shaped like a tiny rosebud. She gave Daisy a gentle squeeze and placed a soft kiss on her powder puff cheek.

*   *   *   *

That night, when Elizabeth went to check on Daisy, she stood at the end of the crib and watched her sleeping. Her breathing was quieter than the gentle breezes around the Keeper's House. "Calm as a dill pickle, still in the jar," Nana would have said. Then the baby squirmed a bit and scrunched up her hands and opened them; her little feet kicked out, then in. Elizabeth patted Daisy's back and began to sing softly in her pure, confident voice:

> *Now the day is over; night is drawing nigh.*
> *Shadows of the evening, steal across the sky.*
> *Savior, give the weary, calm and sweet repose;*
> *With Thy tenderest blessing, may our eyelids close.*

Acknowledgements

There are many people to whom I am indebted for their help in writing this book. I am grateful for their time, advice, suggestions and support.

Dr. Philmore Wass and his sister, Hazel Woodward, helped me to understand what life for families on lighthouse islands was all about. Dr. Wass was most generous in allowing me to learn from him in person and through correspondence. Mrs. Woodward allowed me a delightful interview that gave me the essential female point of view about life on a lighthouse island.

The United Society of Shakers at Sabbathday Lake, Maine, gave gifts of time, space and delicious meals in their peaceful company, so that I could create. No author could have been cared for so well.

Anne Greene, Director of Writing Programs at Wesleyan University, pushed me with enthusiasm, as all great teachers do.

Francina Bardsley, Lee Heffner and Margaret Peet, were invaluable for the three E's, editing, encouragement, and excitement. They were my helium balloons.

Many readers, especially Ed and Kathy Green, Marla Rogers, Stormy Bok, Dianne Rowe, Nancy Tafuri, Heidi Brooks, Faith Gavin Kuhn, Sue Giangarra, Marisa Wischmeier, Carol Orr, Connie Pound, Michelle Gabrielsen, and my colleagues at Westover School, particularly Joe and Beth Molder, Jo Dexter and Ann Pollina, gave me the gift of the green light. GO, GO, GO.

Great thanks to everyone at Maine Authors Publishing.

To my brother, Philip Jostrom:

It is difficult to believe that a kid who would not wear shirts with stripes going the "wrong" way, has become a fabulous artist. I love you dearly.

To my granddaughter, Skye Sanderson:

Amazing, and just think what you will be able to do when you are seventeen. I enjoy the way you see things.

To my husband Roy:

Whatever expression of gratitude and love I might leave here for you would never be enough. Your patience and strength always supported me, guiding me forward. You have been and always will be my True North.